To Amy,

With a smile
and a prayer,

— Juliana Gerace

Gem Babies Odyssey

A journey to the discovery of hope

Juliana Gerace

WestBow
PRESS
A DIVISION OF THOMAS NELSON

WestBow Press books may be ordered through booksellers or by contacting:

WestBow Press
A Division of Thomas Nelson
1663 Liberty Drive
Bloomington, IN 47403
www.westbowpress.com
1-(866) 928-1240

Author photo by Rocky Halim Photography.

ISBN: 978-1-4908-0309-8 (sc)
ISBN: 978-1-4908-0308-1 (hc)
ISBN: 978-1-4908-0310-4 (e)

Library of Congress Control Number: 2013913939

Printed in the United States of America.

WestBow Press rev. date: 10/25/2013

In memory of my dear brother Harold.

"The angels keep their ancient places—
Turn but a stone and start a wing!
"Tis ye, 'tis your estrangèd faces,
That miss the many-splendored thing."

-Francis Thompson

Acknowledgements:

This book would not have been possible without the encouragement and patience of Liz Kiszely, who read, and reread it, offering her expert advice and corrections. Those who have you as a teacher are truly blessed, Liz. I am truly indebted to all the kind souls who graciously read it in its initial stages. Joan Terlisner, Evelyn Thomas, Dianne Lundquist, Josh Baker, Barbara Guerin and Genene Shambo in particular gave me the hope that this could be done. It will always be my prayer that the book finds those who need to be reassured of God's infinite love and mercy.

Table of Contents

Chapter One

Sebastian and Mariel

They had met in Boston while both were in college. She studied art and he, journalism. For three out of their four years of studies, they saw no one else. It was first and irrevocable love. They excelled in their own fields, passionately devoted to them and to each other. Each supported the success of the other, ensuring accomplishments they could never have hoped for alone. Now, she would start her first private commissioned portrait business, and he would write for a syndicated news organization. They were on top of the world. It was New Year's Eve and they were toasting when Sebastian pulled out a fine, velvet drawstring bag from his pocket.

Mariel drew a deep breath. He had an uncanny way of surprising her. A *drawstring* bag? Now, what did *that* bode? *Not* the unmistakable small black box? Her heart was beating with excitement.

"Sebastian...what on earth...?"

"I had it made, Mariel. Go ahead and open it."

Her heart leapt to her throat as her eyes landed on the purest, deepest blue hues of what had to be a tanzanite or sapphire stone surrounded by three of the clearest and most dispersive diamonds imaginable. The pear-shaped center stone seemed kissed by the three diamond dewdrops that adhered to it asymmetrically.

"Sebastian... I can hardly believe my eyes! It is the most beautiful ring I have ever seen...." She stammered at the sheer beauty and mystery of the stone. Sebastian had not said anything about his intentions.

He took a breath, poised and ready for the thoughts he had lovingly prepared. Sebastian the writer had crafted descriptive statements to express his profound sentiments.

"Mari, our love is as deep and life-giving as the oceans of the universe. I know that I cannot envision a future without you, and believe you feel the same. Marry me, Mari. Let's seal our love with a sacred promise forever."

Mariel could hardly breathe because of the hot tears of joy that seemed to rush from her heart to her head.

"Yes, Sebastian...yes, a thousand times *yes!*" she exclaimed as she leapt into his embrace.

They decided on a simple wedding, and two months later they married. Life seemed to unfold new happiness every day. They were fortunate to love so much, to be passionate and successful in their endeavors, and to look toward a future they would carve out together.

It was early April, and the trees were just beginning to bud with the promise of spring. While it rained quite a bit, it had warmed up. Birds were returning from their winter sojourns, alive with the anticipation of mating and nest building. Mariel was preparing her canvasses. The morning mist had subsided, and the light would be just right for a few hours of painting. Sebastian's research on human trafficking had caught the attention of several news magazines. He came home early with an offer he knew would be difficult for Mariel to accept. He was convinced, however, that he must persuade her and pursue what could be the crowning achievement of years of research. The public needed to know, and the international community needed to act.

"They want me on assignment in Chechnya for a few months to see if I can identify some of the kingpins in this racket."

"Sebastian, that sounds dangerous. Chechnya seems to be in the news every day with all sorts of violence."

"I'd have protection from the intelligence community I'd be working with and from the U.S. embassy and to some extent, the military. The Chechen crime bosses do not want to draw any publicity to their engine of injustice. I'll be fine, Mari. To pass this up is to leave all that research inconclusive. There are lives in the balance and horrible crimes against children and women. Mari, knowing what I know, how could I *not* press on? I'm really close to a breakthrough, but I need to be there to make it."

This was not what Mariel wanted to hear. He was so convinced and passionate. He was also right about the years of research. For now, his research and her paintings were like their children. They poured themselves unreservedly into bringing them to life. How could she refuse, when he was right about the suffering of so many innocent children, young women and men? She looked away from him, with tears welling up in her eyes at the prospect of separation, even if temporary. In her heart she understood that she had to make this sacrifice with him. After all, they *had* to do it for the children.

She turned back toward him and embraced him.

"Sebastian, I don't know why, but I was privileged to hear and see those gem babies as a child. Whether it was a dream or a portal of some kind, I was privy to a universe filled with stories of unknown innocent children who had been lost and often victimized. They influenced my life more than I can measure. You know that the paintings in my personal collection are done in a feeble attempt to recapture those faces, and somehow tell their stories. Some of those children hinted at violence and tragedy. Even if I had never seen them, we know it's all too horribly true. It seems to be our destiny to do something—our little part—to speak for them. They need us. But this is really going to hurt, Sebastian. I wish there was another way, or another place— *anywhere* but Chechnya."

"Mari, if things go the way I think they will, I'll be home in a few months. We'll talk everyday, I promise. We can video-chat. You can show me your paintings and I can see that face I love so much! I'll have every electronic and online asset and protection the I.T. community can supply. Mari, we could break this thing wide open, and bring the international community down on these crimes. It's long overdue. I feel it too—the destiny part. We're in this together Mari. I could never do it without your support."

They embraced until her tears had played out, leaving her in a numb resignation. The lively chirping of some songbirds broke her melancholy and seemed to promise new hope. Shafts of light played off the wet and slick sidewalks and tree branches, sending sparkles of playful gleams everywhere. Somehow, she'd get through this—*they* would, together.

Chapter Two

The dream, arrested

Their separation was bitter. Mari had to immerse herself in her work just to keep her sanity. She lived for their emails, and the daily video-chats. Sebastian seemed worn out but fervently focused. He was getting close. Hopefully, that could bring him home soon.

While watching the world news online from national and international sources, Mari sighed in relief each day that passed without reports of violence in Chechnya. But June 19th was different.

She first saw it on the BBC. A bomb in the downtown area of the Chechen capital of Grozny had destroyed office buildings. The news fell on her heart like a leaden albatross. There were no further details. A rush of panic seared through her veins like acid. She emailed Sebastian, but he was not online. She telephoned, but the call did not go through. Her head was pounding heavily. Who would know?

Mariel called the news magazine offices. They were on it, but it was too early for details. They could not yet determine the exact location and therefore had no estimate of the blast's proximity to Sebastian's quarters or offices. The embassy did not answer. Mariel did not know who to contact in the military and was overwhelmed at the thought of attempting it.

"Oh God, let him call. Tell me he's safe. Please God...."

When the phone rang Mariel leapt with nerves firing in every cell of her body. Her head felt as though it was about to explode.

"This is Barry at News Break. Mariel is that you?"

"Barry— is he okay?"

"We don't know yet. The good news is there appear to be no fatalities. The bad news is, over a dozen people have been hospitalized. Mariel, the bomb went off right under Sebastian's office."

Gasping, Mariel no longer heard what Barry was saying. She pictured the shards of concrete rubble she had seen on the BBC. Why didn't he call?

"Sebastian—call me! Please dear God, make him call me! " she sputtered silently.

"Mariel...Mariel, are you there? There is more coming over the wire now. I'll call you right back."

The next time the phone rang, Mariel knew it was over. She just knew. The ring was like the tolling of a large bell— with a somber finality. She was about to implode with the dark foreboding that the worst had happened.

"Barry?" she whispered as she recognized the caller ID.

"Mariel...I'm coming over." He sounded shaken. "Give me fifteen minutes." He hung up.

Her thoughts stung as they ran through her mind. Her heart was beating so hard that perhaps it had exploded.

Everything in her seemed compressed into a single thought: No! Mariel was in a whirlwind of turmoil but Sebastian could *not* be gone.... No, of course not!

Fear battled with hope in a chaotic duel. Oh God! Barry was coming because he had heard something... Sebastian had gotten word out somehow. He would be back and this time he would never leave—ever. It wouldn't be necessary. He had brought the story forward and could send someone else because it was getting too dangerous. He'd want to go back eventually, but this time she would *insist* that he stay.

The darkness of foreboding was nearly crushing. She had no idea whether she was talking or just thinking. She felt severed into two pieces—and bleeding.

"God, no! You won't let this happen. I know I could be better and not indulge my dreams so much. I could—no—I *will* help victims of violence... but I must have Sebastian to do it with me. I'll do something great for them tomorrow: Barry will be ready. He'll help me if Sebastian can't come home immediately. I'll hold it together. I'll be strong. I'll just wait it out, like Mom had to do when Dad was in a war zone and communication was so minimal. *She* did it... I'll call Mom. Actually, I should invite her over, especially since I didn't make it home for Thanksgiving. Oh, I'll make it up three times over! I'll do *anything*...but Sebastian has to be okay."

Her racing thoughts seemed hollow. They seemed to have no conviction. Rather, they kept coming like thoroughbreds to the finish line, but she was aware that she couldn't bet on any of them. Who was she talking to anyway? Someone had to be listening who could ease her fears. This was just another vortex of depressing ultimatums. This time, she wouldn't believe them. The worst could *not* have happened.

Then the bell rang. It was Barry *and* Celeste who had a particular way of ringing. Her head was spinning and she paced in interrupted circles.

That was it. Within two hours the U.S. intelligence community had identified five of its own, including the embedded reporter Sebastian Turner who was pronounced dead upon arrival at the Grozny hospital.

Her world was upside down. The unthinkable had happened. Sebastian didn't make it. He was just leaving for a drink with his colleagues when the bomb went off. A terrorist group was claiming responsibility, but that was not substantiated. Had Sebastian gotten too close to the truth and potentially exposing those responsible for abuse and torture? Would she or anyone ever know? She kept telling herself it simply *had* to be a nightmare. She would wake up, and see his face on her computer screen. He would have survived. He would come home. But awakening each day confirmed the severity and finality of the nightmare. Dear Sebastian would not even be viewed in an open casket. The bomb had marred him beyond recognition.

Dreaded Finality

Mariel stood at the gravesite in a stupor. The spring rain went unnoticed in the fog of sadness she inhabited. She grasped the hands of caring sympathizers, not even knowing who she was thanking. She was somehow buried, too. With Sebastian's, her life was in the pit. Roses landing on the casket were landing on her, too. She wanted to throw herself in with him. Living would be impossible without him. The very beating of her heart urged her to join him. Family members and friends held her protectively as the last prayer was uttered and the grieving party was dismissed so that the gravediggers could complete their task.

Chapter Three

Darkness

Had it been a day, or six months? Perhaps it was longer since Sebastian's burial. Mariel could not decipher one day from the next. She let her voice mailbox fill and did not listen to— much less return— any of the calls. Did she eat, take a shower, or paint? Barely. Days washed over days in an indistinct but agonizing mist. Sleep was her only relief, when at last it came.

She didn't drink or take drugs. Neither did she call her mom, his mother, or a friend. Rather, she holed herself up—numbed and deadened to all stimulation—so that she didn't even hear the doorbell when it rang. Finally, her best friend Celeste, who had a key, broke her seclusion and entered the apartment. Mariel hardly stirred at the sound of her voice, or the calling of her name. She stared blankly out the window, looking as though she had not moved in a week. It did not take the family long to realize that she needed professional support and medical help. Mariel was moved to Whispering Winds on the Cape for healing. Her bereavement had left her nearly catatonic, but the medical and psychiatric interventions were going to position her for a complete recovery. It would take time, but healing and restoration were possible. Life would go on.

Interrupted

Mariel did not recognize her surroundings, nor should she since she had never been to Whispering Winds, but the sound of the waves breaking nearby brought her back to Sebastian. They had honeymooned on the Cape. Often they returned for a weekend or four-day holiday. To feel that ocean breeze, and stare out at the waves in the comfort of each other's affections had soothed their work-weary minds and cemented their love and commitment every time they went. It confirmed and renewed everything about their lives, their love, and the passion they felt for their work.

But this was different. Mariel had to face the waves, the shore, and even the horizon alone now. Still, she felt nearer to Sebastian here on the Cape than anywhere. She tried to drift off in memories of past visits— hoping never to wake from them to the cruel reality of their separation.

Violence! How heartlessly, ruthlessly, irrevocably it severs and dooms the living to its cold finality. She was beyond asking God why he allowed such a thing, and why it had to be Sebastian. She was too numb to believe in the pious and pat condolences kindly souls tried to offer. She lived on what seemed like a floating island of solitude— hopelessly adrift in an infinite ocean over which she had no control— indifferent to the visits, concern and interventions of family, physicians, and friends. Like the driftwood—no longer a living thing but a remnant of one from long ago— she felt helpless, soulless, adrift forever....

Colors

An indefinite span of time had passed when, on this particular day, it happened to be perfectly clear outside. The thick cloud system which had spouted two days of rain, had moved on. The sky was postcard blue, with tiny puffs of clouds—like white lamb's wool. Everything seemed in sharp focus and brilliant. Wildflowers dotted the bluffs and the surrounding hills. It was the first time Mariel noticed color again since...the unmentionable had happened.

Vibrant, pulsing color had always captivated her. Mariel looked at the large, beautiful peridot ring her mother had given her when she and Sebastian married. It was a simple ring with so much of a story! Looking at the ring, however, brought her back to the singular story which had been intricately woven throughout her life. It was *her* story; certainly meant to be shared, but always uniquely her own. In fact, as she looked at the play of color that reflected from the interaction of the artisan's facets and the gem's character, she knew it was time to reconnect with the story she had not revisited for some time.

Chapter Four

The Beginning

Traveling back to her childhood, mentally, was not at all difficult. Life then was simple and full of wonder, notwithstanding some painful separations and loneliness. The colors of this day brought her back to that *first* instrument of enchantment, which had opened the world of color and mystery to her.

It all began with a kaleidoscope—that marvelous tool for the imagination. Certainly Mariel prized hers above all other childhood treasures. How many hours it had captivated her youthful fantasies! The seemingly infinite transmutations of patterns and colors had mystified her and triggered her imagination in a way she could never forget. Most of all, it was the single greatest reminder of Grandpa who had given it to her. Dear Grandpa... the kindest, most loving and patient person in the world! The love he showed her lingered far beyond the years he accompanied her as a child and became a legacy that carried her through life. There was that special birthday, long ago....

She was just seven years old. She was sick and mom had kept her in bed all day. Grandpa came to her bedside with the kaleidoscope and the white parchment birthday card with a "diamond" attached to it. It had a picture of a bunny, with a diamond-like teardrop streaming from its eye. She knew it was how Grandpa felt. She loved him so much, and he loved her. She *could* get well again. She just knew it.

His loving visit strengthened her, and the hours in bed were spent blissfully dreaming as she held that kaleidoscope toward the light coming in through the bedroom window. She felt light, and happy. Grandpa's love and concern were translated into embraces of color and magic as long as she peered through it. Since her father was away for months on end, the presence of dear Grandpa brought a security she longed for.

Though Mariel could not imagine it at the time, her grandpa's visit was an indispensable prelude for a far more important episode in her life. This time Mariel was eleven. Lean and strong as she was, she had no doubt that she could get out to the blackberry patch and back with time to spare, before her mother returned. The sun was bright, and instinctively she brought the kaleidoscope along in the basket she carried for the berries. It would be fun to lie down in the field and look through it where no one could possibly see her hidden in the tall grass. Summers were just made for these kinds of dreamy adventures. Little did she realize the kind of adventure she was about to undertake.

It was August and so hot that day that in no time Mariel felt as if she had turned to solid lead. Her head pounded and the oven-like intensity throughout her body seemed to slow the entire universe into numbness. Helplessly, she sank into the tall field grass. Just last year, she had been here with Grandpa. Now the tears that welled up seemed to sear her lids and blind her. He was gone.

Had anyone been near, they would have seen her sway and stagger a bit, until she had folded over her knees and dropped her face near the ground.

"I can't believe that it can be this hot," she thought. Her heart beat in thundering tolls. Oh, how she missed him. Indescribably! How her head hurt and seemed to weigh a ton!

"I've got to find my way to the couch on the porch, and to the cooler, shaded house," she thought. "I guess the berries can wait."

Dizzy, Mariel started in that direction, but reeled and soon enough sank again. Everything was spinning with images that seemed to blur and disappear.

"This is too weird...." was the last thing she said before slipping into the grass. She forgot her surroundings in a feverish reverie. She must have dozed until the heat and pounding in her head reminded her that she was flat out in the middle of the field— almost too weak to get up. She knew she really had to get home. This was bad. Her thoughts weren't very clear. She needed Grandpa or *someone*. No one was home. Mom had gone to Aunt Jean's to pick up the cherries for the Sunday bake sale, and had left (with her coffee mug in hand) that morning.

"What time is it *now?*" Mariel wondered. "Mom said she'd be back by noon or she would call...but...here I am in the grass field." She glanced over the tops of the tall grass, too weak to stand up. It was a discouraging distance to the house. No one was near. No one would even hear her if she did have the strength to call or scream out. Once again, she half crawled and half sank back like a stone. Even a few steps closer would be good. She kept going.

As she finally cleared the field, the green lawn, freshly mown, seemed like a sponge of coolness. She could breathe again. Laying down to rest, she heard *his* voice. It was Grandpa. It *was* him! She cried, and spun. She knew he was near. He didn't touch her or hug her, but he was with her. Dazed and frantic, she picked up the kaleidoscope and aimed it upward. Through her tears, she saw the amazing confluence of color and patterns—at first sharp edged— then blurred. Too weak to hold it any longer, she let the kaleidoscope fall and gasped, "Grandpa! Where *are* you?"

The tears poured out and down her face. She tried to reach out to him, but instead watched her tears hit the grass blades and then the rich dark earth. She was lying on the grass looking at the many green shoots and smelling the fresh earth. Sparkling tears! Whoa! This *was* amazing. As her tears soaked into the soil, they formed like liquid confetti, melting and sending out rays of color as they sank into the earth. It kept happening, too!

"I just have to look more closely," she thought. Neither tears nor water had ever done *this* before. Each color, as if from a kaleidoscope, fell to the earth in laser ribbons, pooling into a prism which refracted the magical colors out of the ground. Digging with her hands and using the key she had tied on her wrist with a ribbon, she was overcome by the whimsical play of light and color.

"Where could the rainbow of dancing rays be coming from and how could this be?" she wondered.

The next thing she knew, she could hear the laughter

of many children. As she dug she seemed to leave the grass and sky and inhabit a new place that smelled just like cold damp earth. The laughing and gleeful giggles got louder and louder, when suddenly coming up and bouncing all around her were rather large bubble-like bulbs, each with an exceptionally happy child inside of it! They tumbled and collided against each other in blissful play. Each time the bubbles made contact, new rays of amazing color streamed out. Mariel shyly poked her finger into one to see if it was real. She found it pliable, but discovered that it did not burst. It was as if the children inside were being tickled when she tried! They bounced and laughed, giggled and tumbled over and over. Pop! One of them gently burst and the most radiant, miniature child was looking right at her.

"We decide when to come out," this extraordinary child stated confidently. "Usually it is when we are laughing so much that we just burst through, but I couldn't help but notice this time that you were looking *at us*. I'd like to know more about you, and so here I am!"

Chapter Five

Was it a dream?

The next thing she knew, Mariel felt groggy and noticed that she had perspired a lot. She was in her own bed, and the early evening summer breeze was gently moving the sheer peach colored curtains.

"What about the amazing colors, and giggles, and children...?" she wondered. "Was I dreaming?" Then she called out: "Mom...! What happened...?"

In a few minutes, her mom was at her bedside.

"Sweetie... you're awake! Now, you just rest, and sip this nice cool mint tea."

"But I don't remember getting here. It was so hot. I felt...dizzy and weak. And then the... children...."

"Now, Mari, you need to rest. You must have fainted. I found you on the grass when I brought the cherries back. You muttered a little, but hardly woke up. You were wet with perspiration, and clearly had a fever. It's a good thing that your Aunt Jean decided she'd like to help me make the pies today. It would have been hard for me to carry you up the porch steps alone. You were one hundred percent dead weight. Whew! I'm going to call Dr. Peterson now and tell him you're awake."

"But...the children...and the colors...." was all she said before drifting off again.

As Mariel looked around she felt she had crossed some unknown threshold. She could smell the fresh earth and feel its coolness as she dug down a little. But where did they go? The children....

As she worked her key around an earthworm she didn't want to hurt and cleared another clod of cool earth, she saw the most amazing rays of red light!

"No way!" she mused in surprise. As she dug, it was clear that she was getting even stronger rays of the most breathtaking color she had ever seen. In the handful of earth she was about to pile on the side, she saw the source of the rays. It was a huge, ruby-like chunk that she was now cleaning off with the hem of her sundress.

"Whoa! This is a JEWEL!"

As if she weren't startled enough, she saw a kind, soft-featured young face smiling at her from the stone. The ruby—crystalline, sparkling, and red like pomegranate seeds melted and poured in a jewel mold—contained the friendly face of a child...a *living* child! The eyes sparkled, and the corners of the mouth communicated the joy of this encounter.

"Uh...what...!" Mariel gasped. "Are you...real?"

Brightly chiming in with an enthusiastic and friendly tone, the child exuded unusual joy and exuberance.

"Yes, I'm real and so are the others. We've been waiting to meet you. The Great Lord said there would be a day when we would see ALL the others, and even...find our mothers."

"Who are you?" Mariel stammered.

"Only the great Lord knows my deepest name, but you can call me...well, what would *you* like to name me?"

After a pause, Mariel sputtered "...Uh... Beauty, I think."

"Really, you really think so?" Now the child's smile was even more effervescent and she seemed to twinkle with delight.

"Yes, I really do. You are the most beautiful thing... er...girl I have ever seen or met!"

"Confusing, isn't it?" Beauty giggled. "You're right—I *am* a girl. Even though you can't poke me or shake my hand, I'm a girl like you."

"What are you doing here?" Mariel inquired as she wondered where they might be.

"I suppose you would call it *getting ready*. You do that where you live, and we do it here," replied Beauty with a sweet glow in her eyes.

"Getting ready—for what?"

Mariel seemed to catch some of the contagious glee which Beauty exuded, and she was filled with happy anticipation.

"For the Great Lord of course! He continually surprises us with more wonderful displays of his great love. Isn't every moment great because you know he's coming?"

"So you have a...king?" Mariel ventured thoughtfully. "What is his name?"

"You mean you don't know him? It hardly seems possible. His kingdom is everywhere."

"Well... I'm not sure I know him...er...his name. I think I've heard of him, though. What *is* his name?"

"We call him the Great Lord. He is really the best!"

At that point, an explosion of the most awesome, jewel-like colored rays burst forth from within the child in new depths of saturation and radiance.

"I hope you don't mind if I ask you this, but how did you get inside this gem?"

"I inhabit this part of the kingdom because of the journey I made to get here. I did not have a long life where you live. My days were frightful and dark, even though the Great Lord would remind me how near he was. I knew he'd keep me safe. Then on what I thought was a terrible day, the day that violence and anger were lashing out around me, the Great Lord picked me up, and carried me in his arms. He said I looked like the most beautiful lamb and he wanted to take me to the most peaceful place. Ever since I looked into his eyes that day, I knew there would be no more pain or fright for me. His love is so deep and so powerful that it even *changed* me. I've never been afraid or unhappy since he carried me here."

"Wow. That is more than cool."

"*Awesome*, isn't it?"

There was a peaceful pause, like a restful calm between them.

"Well, I have to go now, but would you like to meet some of the others?" Beauty offered. Mariel was still trying to absorb the reality of this conversation and could not respond.

"Tell your mom how much you love her, okay? You'll find your way...." And with that Beauty seemed to fade into the marvelous jewel Mariel could not help staring at.

Chapter Six

If not a dream…?

"Mari, Mariel…are you going to open your eyes, ?" her mother asked as she felt Mariel's forehead and gently kissed her.

It wasn't that Mariel didn't hear her, but it just seemed as if her mom was so far away that she couldn't reach her.

Dr. Peterson wasn't alarmed, but he did seem cautious.

"To be honest Rosie, we have a combo here. She has the fever all right. 102 is a hefty fever for a child. It looks like pneumonia…with the congestion, the fever, and the way she's breathing. The only thing that puzzles me is how easily she seems to be handling it. Did you give her a sedative? I was expecting more restlessness, more discomfort."

"No, I only gave her tea and water. I think she got dehydrated outside. She was going down to the berry patch, and instead of taking the longer way along the fence where we've cleared a good path, she seems to have tried to cut across the field. She really wanted me to bake a blackberry pie when I made the cherry ones, and that's my guess about how she ended up with that gash and all the grass cuts. She was flat out on the mowed lawn, but I could see from the burrs on her socks and the recent path through the tall field grass that most likely she went in pretty deep and then turned back. But, did you say *combo*?"

"She got a few bites, along with those cuts. Do you know how she got the gash on her leg?"

"I wish I did. All I can think of is how that field hasn't been plowed for years. Tom and his friends used to play horseshoes there, even used it for target practice. We haven't mowed it since he started deploying again, except for the path. Could it have been one of the rusty stakes still planted, or some broken skeet fragments from target practice? Tom's friends and some teens from down the road used to use it as a short cut to the house when they came to baby-sit. That grass is so tall now, who knows what's out there."

"It could have been a stake from the horseshoes. That's why I'm going to give her this tetanus shot. Does she have any allergies to medication?"

If the play of light and color was any clue, Mariel felt that she must be getting closer. As she leaned down to reach for the clods with the blue tones of light, she tumbled down into the hole she had dug and found herself flat on her stomach gazing into a pool of water. It was like one of those limestone pools that makes the water a transparent aqua blue and green. She could see that the deeper drop-offs were the most amazing sapphire blue color, and that something down there was creating motion in the otherwise tranquil pool. As she put her face nearer and nearer to the calm surface of the lagoon, she heard laughter and giggling, and saw a commotion of bubbles. Excited in the hope that she might find Beauty or her bubble friends again, she leaned so far in that she fell into the lagoon!

It was an easy and safe float downward. She seemed immersed in liquid aqua blue with facets of light dancing everywhere. She discovered children who pitched and dove in spiraling paths through the water, more at home and agile than any porpoise she had ever watched at the aquarium. Not surprisingly, that is where the laughter and giggling came from. It was a game of tag. Each time one of the children succeeded in tagging the other, they seemed to send out a thousand magical bubbles covered in a luminous coating that showed all the colors of the rainbow. The bubbles spun and then dropped, like a thousand rainbow pillows. Since it didn't seem appropriate to interrupt these children, still intent on their game, Mariel let herself float further downward into deeper majestic blue depths, wafting on the soft caresses of the water.

She might have continued further downward, but Mariel decided to make her way to a plateau that jutted out like a welcome parlor in this water world. Here she had a choice. There was something so alluring about the elegant, velvety blue depths, and she had enjoyed her ability to float downward with no breathing problems whatever. This was such a peaceful realm that there was no reason for fear. And yet, as she continued to gaze downward, the blues seemed to deepen to indigo and then a satiny blue-black, until Mariel could not see any light. A short distance on the plateau, she could see a cave that glowed with a new sort of illumination. It was a simple choice. The light drew her as she recalled that each time she followed it she had encountered the most wonderful new friends.

As Mariel neared the cave and was hoping to hear laughter, she was surprised instead to hear a kind of drone. She stood still. It was a strange noise. Was it the swishing of something huge and unnamed? Pausing to consider whether it was wise to continue, she noticed a few of the luminous, pillow-like bubbles at her feet. As she reached down, she discovered that these too were gems of a most unusual sort, each with uniquely patterned colors. Soon enough as if playing hide-and-seek, faces of lovely, friendly children shone forth.

"Hi," a cherub-like face called out. "It's nice to meet you. Do you like our realm?"

"Oh, yes," said Mariel. "It is better than any game park or aquarium I've ever been to, or even imagined. It's even better than the best movies of the most magical places! I feel safe here."

"It's more than safety you feel. It's love bathing us and washing us, holding and caressing us. What could be better? Each of us here was once like you. When we lived in the other realm, we too were drawn to the beauty of the water. We did not understand the power in that realm, and when we fell in, we came here instead. You still belong back there. We no longer do."

"You mean that you... *drowned*? Mariel said with a gentle shudder.

"We went through the passage. Speaking of *passage*, take me with you into the cave. It will be fine."

Mariel wished she had thought of that before. She could have collected these magical gems as she went along, but until invited to do so she hadn't even thought of it. Luckily, she had a pocket where she safely put the gem and entered the cave.

"Oh! It's an ice cave...or something," she exclaimed.

The cave was lined with pearly lacquer which made it look like milky, iridescent ice. The farther in she went, the more beautiful the lacquer became. She had never seen pearls as beautiful, and there were different hues! Added to the swish and drone sounds were the unmistakable squeals of delight now! These children slid along the edges of the cave like carefree bobsledders. The pearly coat became their royal outerwear, and its slickness gave them an easy ability to shoot around the tubes of the cave like streaming rainbows.

Mariel wanted so much to be one of them. It was incredibly adventurous and exciting. Her musing was interrupted by the voice from her pocket. The *gem baby* was calling her.

"Mariel, your mother needs you. Make sure you give her our love. She's calling you now. Give her our message."

Chapter Seven

Rosie's tears

Mariel's mother had been crying. She was sorry that she didn't take Mariel with her that morning. None of this would have happened. How could she have been so careless? She was also angry. After all, hadn't she always been protective, even to a fault, as her sister Jean had often said? How could it be that the one time she eased up...? After all Mariel had always taken instructions well and been honest.

As she cried and blamed herself, Rosie forgot that Mariel had begged to stay home. She had told her mother that she was so sleepy that she just wanted to stay in bed, and probably wouldn't wake up until her mother returned. Rosie also forgot how many times since Tuesday Mariel had wanted to go down to the berry patch, and how the present heat spell just happened to pick *this* day to bear down on them like a swath of invisible fire.

Rosie was worn out from keeping watch, but luckily her sister was in the house and could manage the baking. It made the house even warmer, however. When would Mariel's fever break? Mariel did not wake up, though she muttered things now and then, and showed the sweetest subtle smile as she slept. Rosie wished her husband were near, but as a medical professional, he was serving the troops in the newest conflict very far away. Her sighs for him always brought her to prayer. It was her absolute helplessness that led her to think of God.

"I need to pray for *her*, my little girl," Rosie thought. "I don't like the looks of this, and Lord, you've **got** to help her...."

She poured out her heart to the Lord, in waves of audibility as well as silence:

"Mariel, my dear little Mariel...! Please...help Mariel, Lord. You can't take her away, not like this....No...not *my* Mariel please...."

Her thoughts wandered to an earlier time when she had lost so much. Muffling her heaving sighs and sobbing now with the tissues she went through, Rosie continued her prayerful pleading.

So far away, and wonderful

Perhaps it was the sobbing that drew Mariel closer to coming back from her feverish odyssey. While she was still in the mysteriously loving kingdom, she was surprised by the sound of her mother's voice seeming to call for her. When the calling became so muffled that she no longer heard it, she found herself whisked away to a wonderful meadow. A thousand dewdrops lingered as opening buttercups sweetly shone in the light. Each small flower sent out what first appeared to be a ray but was in fact more like a cherub inhabiting crystalline shards of golden light.

"More of the *gem baby* children!" Mariel thought excitedly.

As she studied the playful unfolding within this new scene, she saw that each cherub—or each child—carried a fire blossom drawn from the light of the buttercup. The fire blossom sprayed silky, golden threads of light which landed like kisses and warmed her face.

In the midst of this enchantment Mariel found herself carried up and away by these cherubs with their fire blossoms, bathing her in rays of light like ribbons of air. This time she too was swathed in the phenomenal ribboned highway, sliding along the chute of golden light. Each turn and bounce was alive with glittering sparks that tickled and made her laugh. It was all too wonderful!

As she noticed the golden hues deepening into rich, fiery oranges undulating with copper tones too beautiful to describe, she called out to the nearest child, "I'm Mariel! Who are you and who are the other children on this wonderful flight?"

"We are the children whose first light was in the Great Lord's kingdom. Mariel, you'll be leaving us soon, but we'll meet again. Do not forget us, and if you believe in the love of the Great Lord, tell our story as long as you live. The kingdom is alive, within and outside of you, with so many realms and regions. No passage is to be feared. Never leave or turn from the Great Lord. We'll meet again."

Chapter Eight

Return

Drawn back to her surroundings by the tinkling of wind chimes from the outside porch, Rosie left her prayer and decided that she must bake at least *one* blackberry pie. Distressed and at a loss for what else to do, she decided to ask Jean to take her place at Mariel's bedside, and to turn the oven off for a while to cool the house down a bit.

Taking one look at her sister's bloodshot and puffy eyes, Jean could only sympathize with a hug.

"I'd like to pick some blackberries so that I can bake Mariel's favorite pie. Who knows, the aroma from it could bring her back to us sooner. I'll take the jeep and be back really soon."

As soon as the unmistakable fragrance of blackberry pie filled the air, Mariel seemed to stir. Rosie was holding a freshly baked pie right under Mariel's nose so that the scents beckoned to her. It worked like a charm. Mariel's eyelids fluttered and she drew in a deep breath.

"Mom...is that you? Where *am* I?" Mariel whispered weakly as she opened her eyes for the first time in hours.

"Oh, Mari, yes, I'm right here and guess what I have for you? Smell that aroma—your favorite— blackberry pie!"

Covering her with kisses, and making sure that the pie was right in the path of the evening breeze, Rosie was relieved that Mariel's fever had finally broken.

"Mari, let me give you some water. It will cool you off a bit."

After sipping, Mari scanned her surroundings looking perplexed.

"How did you find me, Mom? I heard you calling, but you were so far away, and I couldn't see you."

"Find you? How could we *miss* you slumped on the lawn like a lost parachute? Aunt Jean and I brought you in. You've had a terrible fever, but the worst is over now. You had me worried, though."

"But Mom, where are the children? How did you come down into the earth to find me? You saw them, too, right?"

"There you go again about the children. Mari, I'm not sure, but it seems you had a dream about some children. Do you want to tell me about it?"

"It wasn't a dream, Mom. It was real. When I was feeling sick from the heat, I sunk down on the grass and somehow fell down *into* the earth where I entered a magical underground. There were marvelous gems—blue, and red, pearly, and golden—oh, they were amazing! But even better, each of the gems was really a child. They somehow lived in the gems!"

"...children *alive* in the gems, Mari? Tell me more, sweetheart," Rosie asked pensively.

"They were all so happy. They played and flew and

spun in the most amazing way! Mom, I've never seen more beautiful faces, nor imagined a happier place!"

"Did they talk to you, Mari?"

"Oh, yes! They talked about the Great Lord and how much he loved them. He had rescued each of them and taken them to this magical place. It was a little hard to understand because there was no sadness or pain there, but it seemed to me as if they had lived up here like us, then died and went there. One told me she fell into water, and woke up in *the realm.*"

Rosie had begun to cry. "Keep talking, sweetheart... it does sound so beautiful. Keep sipping the water."

"That's right, Mom! I was *supposed* to tell you! They kept telling me to go to you and to tell you about them! They wanted you to know that they were with the Great Lord who loved and protected them!"

Sobbing now, Rosie was hardly able to say a word. "Oh... Mari....that is so beautiful!"

"But, Mom, why are you crying? It was so happy there, so peaceful. I felt the love. You could actually float and fly in it, and it seemed to hug me no matter what I did. The gem babies said they were getting ready for the Great Lord, just like us. In fact they told me that while we were getting ready here, they were doing the same thing there. What do you think they meant, Mom?"

"Oh Mari.... This is the happiest day of my life! You are safe and sound, and you are telling me about... gem babies...today, on August 14th! I can't believe it Mari... but you *must* be right. It *has* to be true!"

"It's true, Mom. I saw them, talked to them, and even took them along with me. Mom! Check my pocket... I should have some of the gems in it! Where's that summer dress I was wearing? And Mom…what is so special about August 14th?"

"Mari…your summer dress doesn't have a pocket any more, sweetie. You must have torn it off in the fields or something. About August 14th…well, Mari, I never told you because I didn't think you were old enough, but the time has definitely come to tell you now. Remember when you were younger and you wanted a baby sister? Well Mari, you had one. I was expecting a baby, but lost that baby in a miscarriage, six years ago today. *Today*, Mari. I have prayed for little Gemma…(yes, Mari, I named her *Gemma*) and I've prayed every day since I knew I was going to be a mom again, and more so since we lost her. It was very hard for me, but I had to believe that she was with God. Where else could an innocent child be? And now you tell me that children who talk to you out of gems are with the Great Lord! Mari, do you see? It's your little sister, Gemma, and a few others, I guess! They are with our precious and loving Lord, Mari. They are…," she choked, while hugging and kissing and *covering* Mari with her caressing.

A few moments later, Mariel's imagination was churning with new wonder and excitement. She felt a thousand questions well up inside her.

"Wow, Mom, I had no idea…a little sister named Gemma! That is totally amazing! It must have been so hard for you, Mom, and I just never had a clue. Is that why you called your ring…*Gemma*, Mom?"

"That's right, Mari. Your father gave me that ring. Peridot is the birthstone for August babies, and little Gemma was born into heaven in August. He gave it to me so that I would remember that my "precious jewel" would never be lost, and that I would see her again after keeping her close to my heart. Mari, when you get older, I'm going to give you that ring. I never dreamed that your fever could hold such treasures of truth and mystery, Mari, and how I thank God for you and love you. Mari, Mari, my sweet Mari.... You must never forget this day, and keep telling the story...."

Chapter Nine

Shifting Winds

She had been on the Cape for six weeks so far, and although the doctors and attendants were hopeful, she showed little sign of engagement or connection to anything around her. Oh, she could comply when they wanted her sleeve rolled up, or to choose between coffee or tea when they offered, but she always did so inattentively. They had reduced her medication to insignificant levels now, and soon would discontinue it altogether, but still they waited for that "turning of the page," when she would intentionally decide to pick up her life where it had so brutally left off. This particular day she surprised them all by requesting that she be allowed to walk through the meadow and adjacent shoreline *alone* for the afternoon. She wanted to take a sandwich and some water along with a mat, and set out toward the property's end where the jetty would remind her to turn back. Since she would be observable from the second floor balcony, the doctor granted her wish as long as someone kept the binoculars on her the whole time. She was reminded that if she ventured out of sight, she would be accompanied back immediately. Mariel agreed.

Her long flowing summer dress swathed by the gentle sea breeze added to the feeling of freedom and flight she distinctly experienced. How long it had been since she *distinctly experienced* anything! But today, she could see the blueness of the sky reflected so beautifully in the water, with sunlight dancing like confetti on and over the waves in the gentle dance of ebb and flow. It was as if her soul had breathed its way back into the shell of her being, and almost as if... she paused breathlessly as she thought of it... as if Sebastian were near again.

The sun warmed her face, and the fresh and rich sea breeze filled her lungs and sharpened her senses, her mind—everything! Something had just changed. This day sparkled with the kind of magic she remembered in her happiest days, and yet she was perfectly aware that she was alone. Sebastian would not be joining her to skip along the playful waves as they caressed the shoreline. Nevertheless, she did not feel oppressively alone. He was present in spirit, and she knew it! After blanketing the lunch parcel in the mat, and fastening the shoulder strap to hold it, Mariel cast the mat over her shoulder and took to running and prancing on the shore! She smiled for the first time in ...an eternity, it seemed. She felt the teasingly cool water tickle as it sprayed her and soaked the hem of her dress.

She was alive! Not blissfully alive, but poignantly and hopefully alive! And for the first time she could remember since the unmentionable had happened, it was enough!

Exhausted by her sudden exhilaration after having been sedentary for so long, she knelt on the sun-licked shore, spread out her mat, and lay in the warmth of this glorious afternoon. She positioned herself to do what she had not done for so long. She rested her cheek on an outstretched arm and examined the ground in its magical and miniscule detail! Scooping some of the sand, she let it sift through her fingers, and once again saw that beautiful ring— so alive with color and sparkle in the sun's light. The blue sapphire (Sebastian knew that she needed the durability of this superior stone) showed such elegance with the royal blue and cobalt hues which flowed like tides over the face of the stone. The diamonds—bright enough to seem alive with motion, glistened spellbindingly so that Mariel thought she heard the tinkling of triangles and the playful arpeggios of the piccolo and flute!

It's hard to know how long she stared at it, but slowly it inebriated her in its kaleidoscopic play of color and geometric dispersion of light, while the warm sun conspired to calm and soothe her. Soon enough she was dozing. In her quasi dream-like state she seemed to be bouncing along the leaping rays of light and color where once again, for the first time in a long time, she heard his voice! It was Sebastian!

Could it be?

Was it possible? It was unmistakably *his* voice—so warm and present. Though dreaming she was aware that things had changed, and that if he was near, it had to be in a different way. But she could not see him. He had called her name, and she could feel his presence, but nothing more. Moments later, the incoming tide awakened her with a wave so near that the spray of the foam fell on her cheek like the back of a very soft and caressing hand.

What had just happened? Sitting up and getting her bearings, she felt sadly deprived in waking as the sting of her solitude and separation returned. Tears welled up in her eyes. It was almost cruel to have felt him so near, and now so elusive. What kind of trick was her mind playing on her on this particular day which had started out so full of light, and color and engagement with life? She had almost begun to feel like herself again, and now, in spite of the picture perfect day, a pall of shadow had fallen over everything again. Tears began to sting as the pangs in her heart pulsed relentlessly.

Soon enough her head was pounding too. Perhaps the sudden exhilaration along with the sun and excitement of feeling alive, was too much for her. She picked herself up wearily and dragged her mat beyond the tidal line where she could safely collapse in the warm sun. She had neglected to eat or drink anything before leaving and now was forgetful of the food and water she had brought. Tears, along with the aching in her head and heart overtook her, and in the warm sun she again fell into dozing.

The first image to come to mind was that of her lovely engagement ring. She felt immersed in the velvety cobalt blue with undertones of light and warmth from the magnificent pear shape cut, so richly faceted. It was as if the sapphire poured out in liquid form like a fountain that kept flowing until it carried her to the nearby Atlantic. She felt the supporting ripples of ocean currents as she sank into the blues, intermittently illuminated by the three diamonds which gleamed like the beckoning of a light house. The hammock-like arms of a kelp field, undulating with the current and tides, slowed her down, rocking her back and forth in a hypnotic rhythm of calm and serenity.

"Mari... it's me..." became audible in the familiar but perfected tones of her one and only ever love, Sebastian.

"I've made the passage, Mari. I'm safe. I too am in the realm and can see the gem babies any time I desire. But it is you I long to see. You must know that I am at peace, and yes, still very much in love with you and near you—always. I have asked the Great Lord to keep a special eye out for you, as I do also, but you are never out of his sight and love, you can be sure."

Beside herself with joy, Mariel turned this way and that, looking for her beloved Sebastian.

"I know that you can't see me, not yet that is, Mari. But know that I am here, and that I am with you every day. I patiently waited for you to be well enough to return here, Mari. I have a message for you and will help you to realize it. You must visit more of the realm and continue to tell the stories, Mari. These children, and there are others who are older, are like our very own. They disappeared unknown and unclaimed, but we will be sure that their story is told so that others will be safe."

"Sebastian...there is so much I want to ask you, and...." Still somewhat overwhelmed and ecstatic at this reunion of soul and heart with her loved one, she could hardly get the words out.

"Patience, Mari... there will be answers in time. For now it is enough to know that I made the passage successfully and am in perfect peace. The Great Lord will make all things right one day, and reveal how he brings goodness even out of the nothingness of evil. Until that day, he exercises his mercy and love to all who revere him, and even allows the desires of those who refuse his love, as they insanely prefer to be separated from him."

"But Sebastian, why did you have to go and leave me?" Mariel stammered anxiously.

"Patience, my love. In time, all will be made known. For now, you have much to do. I'm going to lead you further in the realm. Remember the darker and deeper waters you did not venture into long ago, when you decided on the illuminated cavern instead? I'm going to lead you there. Do not be afraid of anything you may see. Nothing can harm you, although it may appear frightening. I will be with you, and the Great Lord will not allow you to be overtaken. Are you ready, Mari? We have been selected to do this, together."

"As long as you are with me Sebastian, I will go anywhere and do anything... just don't leave me again—ever!"

"It's time to begin now, Mari. Just follow my voice and look at your ring for light."

With that Mari easily tumbled out of the fronds of kelp which had held her gently resting in the magical sapphire waters. She sank effortlessly and painlessly— again experiencing no difficulty breathing and seeing with distinct clarity.

"Sebastian, couldn't you just hold my hand, or something? It would be so reassuring...."

"Just look at your ring, Mari. You will see my smile, and hear my voice, dearest. The light will comfort and calm you. Just keep it near and in view at all times."

Awakened

"Mariel, you've fallen asleep and the sun is setting. It is time to go back." It was Jack, one of her attendants along with Emmy, a nurse from Whispering Winds.

Groggy and disoriented, Mari could object only weakly: "Sebastian...?"

As she rubbed some of the sand from her eyes, and licked her salty lips, Mariel realized where she was, and though disappointed and exhausted, complied as they lifted her on her feet and then to the dune buggy on which she would ride back to Whispering Winds. Jack and Emmy couldn't help but overhear Mariel as she muttered:

"It *was* Sebastian. I know it was Sebastian."

Exchanging sympathetic glances, the attendant and nurse commended her on her day out, and reassured her that she was making great progress. As to her having a dream about Sebastian, they seemed neither surprised nor encouraging. Neither said a word about that.

Chapter Ten

Life as usual?

"Come on Mari, I'm taking you shopping," came the ruling from Rosie as she looked at Mariel's drab wardrobe. "You haven't bought anything new for quite some time, and it shows. You're home from the Cape, turning over a new leaf, and we need to get you into some new clothes. Come on, it will be fun."

"Mom I don't really need anything. I'm going to return to painting, and jeans and oversized shirts are fine. Really...."

"Nonsense, you've been home over a month and you look shabby when you should be maximizing your assets. After all, you're young, attractive, talented *and available...*"

"We've been over that before mom. I'll never love anyone but Sebastian, and I'm not going to put myself out there. Please mom, I'm an adult, and I know what I want and don't want. Let's not talk about it anymore."

"But Mari, at least some new clothes for a fresh start.... Let's hit the mall and then stop for lunch. If you insist on not having anything new for yourself, I still need you as my fashion advisor. Your artistic flair has always served me well. Besides, I love the fall and winter colors. Sweetie... what do you say?"

"Oh mom, you are relentless and I might as well go or you'll wear me down until I *do* say yes. I'll give you my opinion as usual, but I am not trying anything on. Not a thing, okay?"

After a little spree in which Rosie purchased a new fall blazer, some light sweaters, slacks and shoes, they went to their favorite bakery café.

"I've always loved the cheddar broccoli soup here. What are you having, Mari?"

"I'm not really hungry, but I guess I'll have a latte and bagel."

"...with some strawberry cream cheese, *at least*, Mari. You didn't have breakfast either, and your clothes are hanging on you like sacks where they used to fit. What's it going to take, Mari? You have a whole life ahead of you, if only you'd jump in!"

"Wow, talk about a jump—from cream cheese to my whole life! I'm in, mom, but I have to take it slow. It's still quite an adjustment accepting a future without Sebastian."

"Mari, Mari, my beautiful and talented girl...," Rosie mused as she held Mariel's head between her two hands. She couldn't help but notice that her once chestnut and coppered tresses seemed dull and lifeless as they spilled out randomly under a baseball cap. Those amazing blue eyes were listless and without their usual sparkle, and her beautiful cheekbones were all too sharply chiseled by her recent loss of weight.

"Yes, sweetie, it's true that Sebastian is sadly gone. But there will be someone else. Why just yesterday...."

"Mom, let's go. I really can't talk about it. I'll get the bagel to go."

"Okay, Mari, I'll drop it...for now. But life *does* go on Mari. In spite of your father being in combat zones, at least I had him alive long enough to see you begin college." There followed a lifeless sigh, and an empty gaze as Rosie seemed to zoom out of the present moment. Sitting up straight and taking a sip of coffee, she recovered and continued: "You had barely *a year* with Sebastian. All I ask is that you be open to what may unfold. That's all. Life comes in multiples of 365, and each day is lived once, without our knowing how many we or our loved ones will have. I want you to be happy baby, and loved as you deserve. Really, Mari, that's what I want for you."

Conflicted with empathy for what her mother had endured, Mariel didn't want to end this conversation harshly, but everything in her wanted it ended. The intense resistance she felt when anyone suggested that she could somehow move on from Sebastian brought on a turmoil she could not abide. Yes, her father had been killed by a roadside bomb on the way to assist other wounded soldiers in a temporary hospital in Afghanistan. Her brother, the only son— had died in a helicopter crash while training at Camp Pendleton. Violence had shadowed her family all too closely. Certainly, her mother knew what tragic loss was. She also had to accept the traumatic fracture of her daughter's happiness. In a conciliatory tone, Mariel just wanted at least to *pause* any further thought or discussion on the topic.

"I'm fine mom. I think I'll get a puppy. Let's go to the animal shelter, okay?"

"Okay, Mari. If you want to change the subject, I understand. Maybe a puppy would be good for you. At least you'd get out a little every day. So many young adults are out walking their dogs everyday and... yes, it sounds like a good idea! Sure, let's go after lunch. But Mari, do they allow pets in your apartment? I didn't think they did."

"You're right mom. Let's forget it. But, can we leave? I'm really tired."

Chapter Eleven

Driven

Mariel was clearly driven. She threw herself into her painting and had little interest in anything else, despite all the attempts at matchmaking and social networking from friends and family. She worked around the clock so that she thought of little else. When friends came to visit, her hands and nails were covered with paint, her hair awry, her face worn. Although she was not accepting sittings and worked only on her private collection, she was working too hard, and refused to listen to anyone who told her otherwise.

Family and friends brought Chinese take-out, or pizza, lasagna, ice cream, tea and scones— anything to make sure that she was eating. She did not understand it herself. Every day she awakened, she promised herself to eat, but the day seemed to whir by and aside from vast amounts of coffee or tea, with an occasional piece of bread or scone, she forgot entirely to eat. Finally, each day ended with her yielding to exhaustion— asleep on the now paint-stained sofa, with her coat wadded into a pillow, covered with an afghan her friends had made to remind her of their concern. It was winter and days blurred into nights.

Winter Chill

On an especially cold night, Mariel fell asleep before closing the windows which she had opened to ventilate the studio's paint fumes while she showered. A frigid blast of snow blustered in from the open window. Mariel awoke and struggled to close the ice crusted window. She was in one of Sebastian's flannel shirts, still sweating from the purging shower she had taken in an effort to clean up. When at last she secured the window, she could not shake off the chill she felt. Even under the heavy afghan, her core seemed iced and frozen. Her teeth chattered, and she was too weak even to entertain getting up to put the kettle on. Shivering into a feverish sweat, Mariel felt her body slip right through the couch as if it had been moss over a sink hole. The next she knew she floated into a gel-like pool of cobalt blue and continued the gentle descent downward. Even in her dream she felt cold, but she welcomed the hope that she might just be returning to the realm of the Great Lord, and hopefully, to Sebastian.

"Mari…" It was a tender whisper. "Mari darling… it's me, Sebastian. I've been waiting for you. Mari, you've got to listen to me. You must take better care of yourself. It is not for you to rush your arrival here. You are here now, but it's only temporary and there is no telling how much time we have. Follow my voice, Mari, and look at your ring. It will cast a light that lingers on your immediate surroundings until we get to the cove of lights. Are you ready Mari?"

"Sebastian, oh Sebastian...! I've missed you so much. Of course, I'll do anything, and go anywhere with you. Don't leave me Sebastian...."

With that she dove through the sapphire gel. It slipped around her limbs like the silkiest compress of sweet smelling minerals and herbs one could imagine. It strengthened Mariel immediately. Breathing and seeing were once again unimpaired, and she relaxed as if she had been born in this magical environment.

The mystical blue gel began to pulse with an opalescent light which grew brighter and brighter. It was then that Mariel noticed that she no longer needed her ring for light. Every swell and flow of the blue gel caused an iridescent glow of streams and bubbles. The motion of their own movements added to the brightness of the mixture, and they began to hear the most wonderful choir of sweet voices. "The King of Love, my Shepherd is...." While unfamiliar to Mariel, the hymn was offered in the most amazing and nuanced harmonies.

"It's the cove of lights, Mari. They've been expecting you."

Before Mariel could ask who *they* might be, she turned past a coral-like wall, and came face to face with what seemed to be hundreds of smiling faces—aglow with the purest joy as they sparkled with the anticipation of having visitors.

"Oh Sebastian... they are beautiful—and their voices!"

The cove of lights was lined with what looked like the

interior of a giant geode. The walls were covered with sapphire crystals— each containing a uniquely beautiful child's face. They were free to move from crystal to crystal, and did so with the utmost delight as they bounced and spun in playful glee.

"Mari, listen carefully. I know this is like a dream, and when you return there will be many who will say what you experienced was the result of what is probably a pretty high fever by now. But remember, *they* are real. That is what I'm here to remind you of. They need a voice—our voice. We were painfully separated, but only so that I too could visit the realm you experienced so long ago. These are the innocent, largely anonymous faces of those lost in the terrible injustice of slavery, abuse, and violence. Human trafficking, Mari, is unfortunately alive and prospering. These innocent souls are only a few of its victims. Now, Mari, they will be *our* children—the fruit of our love and labors. I was so close to exposing one arm of this operation. Now it will be up to you, to help make them known."

"Sebastian, what can *I* do? This is unbelievable...and a bit overwhelming."

"I know Mari, but you *are* up to it. It will be a way for us to stay united even while apart, and I'll be prodding you as much as I can. Remember, Mari, this will be the fruit of *our* love. They will be *our* children. Tell their stories, Mari by painting their faces. Your gifts can be the vehicle to draw attention to their former pain. Continue to paint them as gem babies—as many as you can remember. Each gem is a monument to an invaluable life snuffed out. Let the world hear from them through your painting. Mari, you must...."

A sudden hush came over the entire cove. The faces within the sapphire crystals faded. A murky ink began to fill the cove.

"Mari, look at your ring, and do not be afraid. You cannot be harmed. I told you that evil would try to block you by instilling fear. It is as ugly and insignificant as that inky cloud. It will follow you and try to scare you. It may take on monstrous faces, but do not be deterred. The truth is more powerful and will dispel that cloud the way the sun disperses darkness each morning it rises. See...it is dissipating now, because of the truth in what I'm saying. It is only a vapor— an illusion, and has no power over the Great Lord and those whom he protects."

With that the myriad of faces began giggling and peeking through the sides of the crystals—unharmed and as blissful as ever. They spontaneously broke into a chorus of praise for the Great Lord and the peace of his realm.

"Mari, darling.... You have to go back now. Do not forget what you have seen. This is just one part of the realm and as you know, there are so many others. Adolescents, teens, and women are victimized and must be given a voice and a face in your world. Take care of yourself Mari, so that you can continue painting. Each face is a child of ours, Mari. I'll be with you as you recreate each one, and remember Mari...we'll be together again one day."

"Don't leave me Sebastian.... It's too soon and I can't make it without you...." Tears began to flow from her eyes, turning the opalescent blue into rainbows of colors which streamed into flowing patterns as she turned to find him.

"Go back, Mari. We'll meet again. Take my love with you and paint...*our* children, Mari. The fruit of our love...."

The distant tones of that beloved voice grew fainter as they got farther and farther away.

Without trying Mari could feel herself rising upward. Leaving the luminous cove area and the swirls of light within its confines, she re-entered the cobalt blue gel, with its healing powers. Effortlessly, she was lifted until she broke through the filament which divided the realm she had just left from the reality of her studio apartment on that cold winter night. Still half asleep, she began to recognize the signs of having returned. An ambulance siren split the quiet of 3 AM in the ever pulsing city.

"What on earth could be in its way at this hour?" she wondered, as she realized that she was growing quite alert.

She felt the excitement of a new challenge and realized that each time she took up her brushes she now would be connected to her beloved Sebastian. She felt warm and invigorated, and was actually hungry.

Chapter Twelve

A New Start

Bounding off the couch, she made some coffee and inserted a frozen bagel into her toaster. Her melancholy seemed to have lifted. She felt whole and healthy again. Even at this pre-dawn hour, she was anxious to clean up her studio and begin painting while those faces were fresh in her mind.

Looking for butter in the refrigerator was like digging in a landfill. The cluttered storage of various meals in still unopened restaurant containers, made it impossible to find anything. She took a large trash liner and tossed everything out, discovering rotten fruit and vegetables wedged in between, along with curdled milk and half opened pints of yogurt. As soon as it was light she planned to restock with healthy, fresh foods. In the meantime, she had to do the same to her apartment which was lined with old newspapers, coffee stained magazines, wrappers, overflowing wastepaper baskets, and piles of unwashed laundry. This was a new day! She looked at her ring, and this time she smiled back to the tears of joy that were in ready supply.

By the time the sun rose and morning traffic began, Mariel had washed and dried three loads of laundry which she placed in plastic bags, ready for donation. It was time for a change, and if she was going to get out there, she needed to look alive and well.

"Mom was right", she thought. "Wait till she hears I want to go shopping!"

It was difficult parting with Sebastian's clothes, even though it had been more than a year since he had left for Chechnya. She decided to keep a few of his long sleeved shirts which made great painting smocks. The rest, hers and his—were all going to Simply Share. So much had happened, so much had changed. She had entered a new chapter of her life and felt stronger, healthier (even if thinner). She was a more hopeful Mariel! It sent her head reeling at just the thought of it all.

"I had better stick to today's plan, and then take it one day at a time. Sebastian will be nearest if I push forward on the paintings," she reminded herself.

Reality

As she opened the box in which her friends had sorted all the incoming bills, Mariel had a cold awakening to the reality of her situation. She had cancelled all her sittings and declined all commissioned jobs during her recovery and bereavement. Sebastian's most recent research was destroyed on the computers that blew up in the explosion, so there was nothing new to publish. Aside from his car, which she sold for living expenses as she downsized to the studio apartment, he had left little in the way of any inheritance. They had worked hard to pay off their student loans. While she had some savings from the insurance policy, she realized that whatever was left over from the funeral would soon be gone when she paid her bills and advertising costs for the gallery exhibition she had postponed when he died. She needed to do something, and quickly.

Never one to ask her family for help, Mariel assessed her collection. So far she had seven lovely gem baby paintings—each in a different hue. She had managed to produce these as her own private hobby. Then, she had about twelve from her feverish painting spell since her return from Whispering Winds. These were distinguished by the sienna, and umber tones she used during this period. And while they did not resemble anything she had seen in the realm, they were her mind's projection of the silent scream which issued from the painful experiences of the abused and enslaved victims of trafficking. The faces were sad, withdrawn and distrustful. Their eyes protruded from hollow faces with the forsaken look of abused or neglected pets and animals. They could be a powerful statement of the injustice to which she wished to draw the world's attention and could very well be a part of the gallery exhibition. They would need to be balanced by the hopefulness and peace she found in the real gem babies. Perhaps she could replicate them in one great mural painting, refreshed and alive in all the brilliant colors of the realm.

Then, she'd need to paint the cove of light and some of the others she recalled but had never painted. As Muriel brainstormed and began to envision the exhibition, one thing became clear: she needed underwriters and soon.

It's time

As she ruminated and planned, her mind went back to each precious word Sebastian had said. These would be their children—very much the fruit of their love and inextricable from the shared purpose of their lives. There *had* to be a way.... Sebastian would help her.

Working on her third cup of coffee—and drinking it black until she could get to the store, she suddenly had a brilliant idea. Why not ask some of the social action groups working on the human trafficking issue if they might consider her work as a kind of logo for the united efforts of their groups? Perhaps through university or private grants, the exhibition could be underwritten, and the profits (after some compensation for herself) from copies of her works sold as posters and stationery—even numbered collectible reproductions—would go to the organizations themselves! Wow! All of a sudden, her paintings were pregnant with powerful potential for advocacy, as well as financial support! This is exactly what she needed to do!

Chapter Thirteen

Pivotal Interview

In the next few weeks, along with re-stocking her refrigerator and kitchen pantry, and buying some new, albeit smaller-sized clothing, Mariel secured three interviews during which she would pitch her idea and show her portfolio. She enlisted a mutual friend of Sebastian's who was a wonderful photographer and who produced a breathtaking portfolio presentation along with her bio, credentials and a logo for the collection: *Gem Babies*. The bio included the tragic story of her beloved Sebastian's work in researching and exposing the network of trafficking in Chechnya, which spread its heinous tentacles throughout eastern as well as western Europe, along with North and South America. The details of her personal and supernatural experiences were known only to Sebastian and her mother, with Celeste privy to a few, and it would stay that way for now.

Setting out in her crisp, new, apple green, tweed suit, deep amber high boots, scarf and purse, she boarded a plane for New York City with butterflies as well as knots in her stomach. Her heart pounded with expectation and excitement. This could be the launch of a powerful new campaign for human rights. In time, it could even come to the attention of the United Nations.

Her first stop was at the *Invisible Crime Center* for Human Trafficking where she was meeting with the founder as well as the media arm of the organization. They were interested in her artwork as a way to garner new interest in a news and advertising world where suffering children's faces had grown stale and overused. Also, the appearance of suffering can unfortunately make some turn the other way because of the painful reminder. ICC had been looking for a fresh approach for some time, but had not come up with anything compelling enough.

It did not take long for a swell of excitement to resonate in the conference room on the fourteenth floor in midtown Manhattan, just minutes away from Times Square. The well known location for the New Year's Eve throngs, though somewhat improved, was still a hotbed of prostitution, drugs, and yes, human trafficking because of the high percentage of teenage runaways who gravitate there.

Steve Irving, executive director and founder of the organization was very enthusiastic. He was a study in contrasts. Wearing a Rolex, and sporting a tweed jacket which looked as though it had been worn for at least a decade, he shook his rather long hair and pronounced his decision with authority.

"Mariel, you are a well known artist and illustrator. I remember a feature article done from an exhibit hosted at Columbia a year or two ago. You drew attention then, and could do so now. The unfortunate and tragic death of your husband, Sebastian Turner is a loss for the world, but his work could be immortalized through you. I think this is a good direction for us. I'd like a contract drawn up for us to host and launch a new advertising campaign for Invisible Crime Centers and use your paintings as our "mascot" of sorts. I know at least five people I could call this afternoon who, on my recommendation, would underwrite the whole shebang without a second thought. Of course, we're a non-profit so their backing would pay for the event, advertising, and provide capital for the initial promotional products. We'll need professional press releases, with a bio on Sebastian and his work on behalf of the victims, and the way your paintings are meant to bring the faces of invisible victims into the spotlight. Mariel, do you have anything that survived the bombing in Grozny from Sebastian's latest writings? That would be invaluable."

"I wish I did. The police are on the take from various factions and criminals there and the whole incident was cleared up too fast. The hospital did not release any of his personal belongings to me, and when the apartment was investigated, it was already cleaned out, with no one seeming to know who had done the cleaning. His computer was gone, along with his journals."

"I might be able to do a little investigating for you, Mariel. I have a colleague from my early days of teaching international law at Columbia who is a liaison with the intelligence community in Grozny, believe it or not. I'll see if we can pay someone to do a little digging. For a price, you can pretty much have anything you want over there. He knows plenty of moles, too."

"That would be fantastic!" Mariel could hardly believe her ears. Perhaps she would recover something of what

Sebastian had discovered before he paid the price with his life.

A buzz of excitement ran through the group like a shock wave. This was going to energize the IC Centers almost to the point of re-inventing them!

"Now, as to the sale of prints and posters of your work, Mariel... I'd like you to meet with our attorney and accountant so that an acceptable contract can be drawn up. We'll need to compensate you for the use of your work, time, and effort with some royalties (I suppose.) The rest of the profit will go to fund our work with the victims. Agreed?"

"Mr. Irving, your offer sounds just fine. However, with all due respect, I have two more interviews lined up this week with other agencies..."

Interrupting with his usual assertiveness, Steve Irving settled the matter quite definitively:

"Nonsense, Mariel! You were smart to come to us first. We are the largest and best known. I'll offer a $5,000 advance over and above all other agreements for an exclusive—and that will come from me personally! I know everyone else out there, so just let Suzanne know who you're supposed to see, and we will personally call them to let them know that you signed with us. If they want to help with the promotion, I'll share some of the proceeds with them. We work cooperatively where lives are at risk, so there will be no problem. What do you say?"

Besides herself with how smoothly everything had gone, Mariel began to feel her worth again and agreed with a handshake and an appointment to see the accountant and agency's attorney. Her financial worries were over, and more importantly, her work on behalf of the abused and trafficked victims would soon be well on its way.

"You are a fine artist, Mariel, and I am honored to work with you and to make Sebastian's work known. Your acceptance of an exclusive enables us to move quickly. I'm hoping for a two month ad campaign and a spring exhibition and launch. We'll have a fundraiser party to go with it all so that we get some of the heavy hitters in here. You'll be very well known after this, Mariel. I'll see that you have your advance, in a few days. How's that? "

Before she could get her words out, he dictated to Suzanne, "Get me Brad Olsen on the phone, over at the *New Yorker*. Tell him I have a hot feature article for him!"

Standing to take her leave, and humbled by the overwhelming response to her work, she stammered: "Thank you Mr. Irving. I'm very grateful and happy to work with you. I also hope that your connection in Grozny might recover some of Sebastian's work. I'll look forward to hearing any results in that regard, and again, thank you."

"My pleasure, Mariel, and you can call me Steve. Gotta run... I'll let you know what we dig up."

Mariel walked to the train station lighter than air. She was truly on her way, and anxious to complete the paintings in her mind's eye of the cove of lights, and others. "Sebastian... you *are* helping aren't you? It all fell into place so quickly and...perfectly. I feel your presence," she reflected. Taking a deep breath, she tossed her head back to look up at the sky before entering the station. She gasped and smiled as she scanned what a skywriter had just completed overhead: *Love You.*

"That's just like you, Sebastian," she thought as a smile warmed her heart and mind.

Chapter Fourteen

Back in the Studio

Undoubtedly there was a new wind in Mariel's sails. She was commissioned and would soon be quite well known. This could lead to a strong career. More importantly, the extraordinary task of illuminating the invisible crimes of abuse and trafficking for which she felt her paintings had been destined would at last become a reality. She felt her life braided once more with Sebastian's in a noble and unbreakable bond.

The canvasses of the cobalt blue motif were only half started, then abandoned. She had been ruminating too much, and now needed to get very busy. They would need her originals at least a month before prints were made. Since daylight was waning and she wanted to start fresh and early, she decided she just had to celebrate all of this with *someone*. Her thoughts immediately went to her best friend to whom she had promised a report on results of each day's appointments.

"Celeste? Want to come over? I've got some good news, for a change."

Celeste screamed excitedly into the phone.

"You're back already, and with good news? I just knew it Mari! It's time for things to turn around for you! I'll pick up some wine and be there in less than an hour. Wooo hooo!"

Mariel's studio was now candlelit, with her favorite music playing and a fresh pizza baking in the oven. Celeste had faithfully visited her every day during the early days of her grief and debilitating shock after Sebastian's death. She had gently affirmed her, without ever pushing her, and had recently noticed that Mariel was determined to get back into life. She just couldn't wait to hear what had transpired at the very first interview!

The two friends loved each other like sisters. When Celeste entered the apartment they jumped and hugged each other like twins long separated.

"Tell me everything, Mari. Spare not a single detail! Pour it on...I'm all ears!"

"Celeste, it's all so wonderful that I actually went out and got champagne. You're always the one treating me- allow *me* to pour some really good news!" It's about time we toasted!"

With that she popped the cork, and poured two full crackled glass flutes.

"To Mari!"

"To friendship!"

"Well, the long and short of it is that Steve Irving from Invisible Crimes Centers wants my work exclusively and is even sending a $5,000 advance to cinch it! He loved my work, and wants a bash, and a huge advertising campaign, with prints and stationery made, along with a coffee table book and next year's calendar!"

"Oh Mari, that's phenomenal. ICC is really the strongest and most prominent of those organizations—isn't it? And wasn't the founder interviewed on 20/20 or something? That must be Steve Irving, right?"

"Oh, yes, that's Steve all right. He's a power house. And Celeste, you haven't heard the best part yet. He has contacts in Grozny and is hot in pursuit of anything of Sebastian's that might have survived the blast. He thinks it highly likely that Sebastian entrusted a back-up disc or flash drive to someone there. Think of it, Celeste. It makes perfect sense. We both know how cautious and protective Sebastian was of his research! He also knew better than anyone how volatile the situation truly was there. Perhaps there was a safety deposit box, or a friend with a back-up drive with some of his more recent information. Steve said this could blow wide open once they have specific charges for the suspects. He was talking about Senate hearings and a book. I'm serious. This guy Steve is like a rhino that will blast through any obstacle. He is so committed to overturning the hideous crimes of trafficking that he will rally people, media, and amazing resources until he is victorious. It's also clear that he knows big money and seems to have assets himself, which he is willing to put up for this exhibition. Celeste, if we recover Sebastian's work from Chechnya and get it in print, his life's work could be immortalized. Celeste, more than anything, I want to find out what he knew, and died for...."

Her gaze became distant, as her voice trailed off. Tears began to well up as she thought of Sebastian, who should be here to celebrate with her. Instead, she hoped for crumbs and fragments of his work that might be found.

"Mari...did I lose you? Come on, this is no time to get gloomy and distant. This whole story has Sebastian written all over it. I believe what you've said before. He is orchestrating and pushing this project from *wherever* he is. It's as if he's ...well, like you've said— still with you."

"Oh Celeste, I love you! That's it exactly. I felt his presence the whole time I was in New York. Then the whole meeting with Steve went so smoothly. It was uncanny. Do you know what I saw right after the interview when I just happened to look up at the sky before entering Penn Station? You are not going to believe this."

"What Mari, tell me...what? I can't stand it...tell me! I have goose bumps all over."

"Cellie, I wouldn't tell this to just anyone. But since you believe me about Sebastian staying close in his own mysterious and loving way, I'll tell you, but don't breathe a word, okay? It's just so intimate and personal. Promise? "

"Mari, I'll chop my arm off for collateral. Just tell me already!"

"I looked up, and just then a skywriter had finished writing LOVE YOU directly overhead!"

Shrieks of delight, followed by sisterly hugs and more toasting sealed the celebratory tone of the evening. Hours whirred by in cheerful chatter and hopefulness after which, notwithstanding Mari's protests, Celeste called a cab and insisted on leaving. In spite of Mariel's reminders of how late it was and how she had an air mattress Celeste could use, her dear friend remained implacable. Intuitive as always, Celeste knew it was time for Mari to plunge herself into this project.

"It's been great, Mar...now go to sleep and wake up

ready to paint as if your life depended on it. Call me when you're ready or if you forget to eat...."

What a treasure her dear friend was. Mariel recalled the many times Celeste had been there when she needed her most, and now Celeste had just confirmed what Mari knew very well in her heart. It was time to hunker down and paint.

Chapter Fifteen

Impasse

The canvasses were primed, the sketches made, and now—an impasse. She couldn't paint. The faces eluded her. Mariel mulled it over in her mind, wondering exactly how much time she had lost that week.

It doesn't make sense. If Sebastian is fine, and the gem babies really represent the spirits or souls of children tragically lost or killed, why is it that I must always *descend* to some lower region to encounter them? She shuddered at the thought of all her experiences being merely a deception of some evil sort and that she had been no more than its naïve and helpless prey. Her thoughts raced again. How can I paint the colors, the beauty and innocence of those faces if that is the case? Why should I play into what is merely fantasy at best, and malicious illusion at worst? I can't do it! My head, heart and hands are not in harmony, and the painting won't flow. Every attempt seems contrived and shallow, and it should be honest and pure. Maybe I did spin a fantasy tale in my mind to cope with the loss of Sebastian.... Oh no...that's it! It was after losing grandpa that I first experienced...or... *thought* I experienced the discovery of the first gem babies. Oh no...what if it's *all* unreal? Was Sebastian's death avoidable? Had he thought that this would be a way of having children to love and devote ourselves to...or did I just make that up in my mind as well?"

The torment continued. As she thought about Celeste being in New Orleans for a week in order to attend her sister's wedding, it occurred to Mariel that today was Valentine's Day, and that she was especially lonely. She didn't have a sister. Her brother was so much older; they had never been close and now he, too, was gone. Sebastian... the mere thought of Sebastian brought with it flashes of involuntary anger and frustration. Why didn't she have Sebastian? This kind of impasse was more than she could handle.

Hearing the door slam behind her, Mariel leapt outside with a brisk step. Her thoughts were spinning like a runaway wheel. What was going to happen now, if she couldn't paint? Was this some kind of cruel fate designed for her once again when she had finally found some happiness? She walked and walked, vaguely aware of her surroundings, but more involved in her thoughts. On the one hand she wished that she could shake all those ominous thoughts, and on the other, she felt that arriving at some answers was all that could free her. Achieving either solution was beyond her. That much she knew.

Her desperate pace and agitated thoughts were interrupted as a young child slipped in front of her and happily skipped up the stairs to two enormous doors. Unable to open the doors by herself, the little girl tugged and tugged, and then began knocking. With a halting start, Mariel wanted to tell the young girl that the doors were so thick that no one would hear her knocking, but decided to try the doors herself instead.

"Excuse me, sweetie. Let's see if I can open the door, for you. You seem to know this church."

With her strong arms, the huge door glided open and the little girl leapt inside. Mariel gave a quick glance at the interior, and noticed that the little girl soon disappeared down a side aisle and behind a niche. Wondering how the child seemed so familiar with these surroundings when there didn't seem to be a parent or teacher nearby, and overcome by the loveliness of the light coming through the stained glass windows, Mariel slipped into a pew and just sat. The frantic pace she had kept until she found herself here seemed overcome by a sense of peace and warmth.

She stared up across and down the magnificent stained glass window before her. If not an actual Tiffany, it certainly had been influenced by his style. The flowers and foliage had that familiar softness so difficult to achieve against the distinct leaden outlines which secured each glass piece. The figure of a woman, perhaps Magdalen at the feet of Jesus, was so composed and alive at the same time it took Mariel's breath away. She had never seen a face so serenely intense—which seemed until now—like a contradiction of terms. There was something about that quality which reminded her of one of the faces in a…gem.

Getting on her knees, she put her head in her hands at the unwelcome deluge of doubts that swirled within her. Her head and heart ached as she grasped to understand what was going on. What was she to believe? Should she paint, and if so, what was holding her back? How was it that she could see a great dream being realized, and then find it dissolved in the murky pain of self doubt and solitude?

Hardly knowing how to pray, Mariel looked again at the window. She identified immediately with the figure at the feet of Jesus. This woman thoroughly acquainted with disillusionment and loss, seemed to draw an inner strength as she looked into his eyes. She was at peace. She knew with every fiber and cell of her body that she was not alone and that her hope was not in vain. Most probably it was Mary Magdalen. The signs of Jesus' wounds showed the time depicted was after his resurrection. Magdalen's torment was over. Jesus triumphs — eternally alive and present. He can and always will be with her. He chooses to answer her prayer when she calls out needing him. In fact, he comes even before she does…. Mariel knew that much of the story from having studied the paintings of Fra Angelico and others.

A warm, reassuring feeling came over Mariel like a soft and cozy blanket. As she closed her eyes and basked in calm and consolation, tears once again found their way down her cheeks. This was the answer she needed. The fact that she had found this church, and had been led to it by a child no less, where the breathtaking Tiffany waited like a quiet friend—all translated into one word: *Believe.*

Her demons seemed to shrink in the light of this moment. Though hope and faith were required of her, it was not illusion or recklessness to hold on to them. In fact, it was recklessness to let go of them and relinquish the unique experiences of her life and the singular mission she shared with Sebastian in life, and yes, after his death.

One question still lingered. Why did she seem to go "down" to a place in order to find or communicate with the gem babies? Traditionally, the "underworld" was a place of the dead, often haunting in its mystery. Even in other great literature, it might be associated with suffering or even hell. Instead Mariel had always experienced unparalleled joy and playfulness, light and angelic music when she "visited."

Rubbing her eyes and forehead as she shifted in the pew and decided to lie down, Mariel was overtaken by a stunning window displayed in a portion of the apse which had eluded her earlier. It depicted the visit of the magi. The background was a deep, cobalt blue, night sky, illumined with jewel-like stars. As she lay back in the pew and relaxed for the first time in a week, Mariel realized that she was a bit lightheaded. The previous seven days were fraught with torment, sleeplessness, and now that she stopped to think about it—almost no eating. Tea and coffee along with stale bagels which she had dunked, were the only nourishment she had taken while in the throes of doubt and creative paralysis. She could almost hear Celeste admonishing her as once again she had neglected the most basic rules of self-preservation. Thankfully, she could turn this around before Celeste returned—as soon as she took up her brushes again. But here and now in this church, enveloped by the most astonishing panorama of simulated constellations and night sky, she was overcome by a trance of drowsiness. It was as if her body, finally free of the tortures and restlessness was screaming for rest and healing.

She gazed sleepily at the magnificent window of stars and blue and was reminded of the gel-like cobalt she had floated in when she visited the realm last. Weakly, she pondered that each time she re-entered that magical place she clearly felt that she was descending. And yet, it was so obviously a place of peacefulness and bliss. She scanned the magnificent panels above her: indigo and cobalt illuminated by pearlescent lights. She allowed her tired mind to drift aimlessly, immersed in the space.

And then, (like a flash of lighting,) it came to her! The cosmos is an expansive and expanding reality. There is no up or down, unless relative to a fixed point and in a one dimensional sense! That would be for the sake of measurement perhaps, but since space expands indefinitely in all directions, truly there was no up or down—only outward immersion! That was it! Epiphany!

Mariel felt illuminated and comforted. While the floating and downward wafting was a comfortable metaphor, perhaps for a caressing safety, it had nothing to do with up or down. She was simply leaving familiar terra firma. She had to be immersed. She had to enter a realm not bound by the physics of this world, and in her psyche this seemed like a downward sinking as if by gravity. And yet, each time she seemed weightless—as perhaps she might be in space or a different atmosphere. And of course it *was* a different atmosphere. When seemingly in water, or the gel-like substance, she breathed comfortably and safely!

Now she felt truly comforted. She had solved a lingering doubt, and it was as if her entire being breathed a unanimous sigh of relief. She felt herself at peace, and was smiling in fact.

"A short nap couldn't hurt," Mariel thought as she recalled the solitude of her surroundings. No one had entered the church since she had opened the doors for the little girl. Lying down as she was in the pew, no one would see her if they did enter. Though intending to sleep she could not take her eyes off the starlit sky depicted in the magnificent glass artwork. The blues seemed to swirl as if stirred, making ribbons of light out of the starry points. As her eyelids grew heavier, she gave into her fatigue in the safety of this sacred place.

"Just a short nap...," she thought as she easily drifted off to sleep.

Like the colors, Mariel felt herself swirling and spiraling downward. Was it a funnel or a wormhole? It was as if she was spinning in the lens of a kaleidoscope, with all the colors racing in liquid circles all around her. Though spinning, she wasn't dizzy. In fact, she was ecstatic. She seemed lighter and freer than she had ever been, and soon enough, she heard the laughter.

"We were hoping you'd come. Your visits in the realm are the most exciting news to all of us. Welcome, Mariel."

The loveliest, dewy-fresh face beamed out of one of the hundreds of moon-like gems around her, each lit with eager eyes of a hundred friendly faces.

"My name is Ari. We have a most wonderful surprise for you."

The excitement and anticipation of the others rose to an elated pitch of chatter and laughter which sent them spinning and whirling in their moonbeams, or "moongems."

"Where *am I* Ari? This is different from the other places...there is no water or soft gel. I feel so light and feathery."

"You are visiting a different part of the realm of the Great Lord. We made our passage through the air, whether from flight or falling and found ourselves gently carried here. Like you, we landed ever so softly—like a feather on a cloud, knowing that we are loved and cherished by the Great Lord."

As Ari finished her statement the throng of moonbabies rose in choruses of the most mystical harmonies imaginable. Then just as suddenly—all was hushed as hundreds of pure, sparkling eyes looked excitedly past Mariel.

"Mari...?"

"Sebastian!"

It was the happiest embrace she had ever experienced. She knew that Sebastian had somehow led her to the church, the enlightenment, and the dispersion of her doubts.

"Did you like the sky writer?"

"Sebastian, that had you written all over it! You are too wonderful. I miss you sooo much!"

"Mari, Mari... we *are* very close. Don't you see—I am always near? That is why I send you little messages to remind you. This time, I have a special gift that you will take back. Look at the sapphire Mari. Take a good long look at it."

"Yes, Sebastian, I love it. It always draws me near to you. But, I don't get it. Is there something different about it? It seems as beautiful as ever, but the same."

"You'll see, Mari, in a while. Now you must hurry back, take care of yourself and paint. I will be with you, like a bird on your shoulder—singing in your ear—keeping you company wherever you go. The faces you see here were innocent children caught in the foul terror unleashed through unscrupulous and wicked profiteers. They were lucky that air travel mishaps prevented them from ever reaching their destinations, since they would have been enslaved and abused. They made the passage instead. Remember Mari, as you paint them, each is a child of ours. Tell the world. Mari, be strong. You can do this. Remember the faces…and know that I am always near."

Just then Mariel felt a gentle nudging.

"Ma'am? Excuse me ma'am. I'm going to lock the church and it will be very dark in here. Perhaps you had better go home. Are you all right?"

The kindly, large brown eyes and gentle voice came from the church sacristan.

Realizing where she was, she sat up quickly and tucked back the hair which had fallen around her face.

"Uh…sorry. I mean, thank you. Yes, I'll go now. I must have fallen asleep. It was so peaceful here," she sputtered as she gathered her scarf and tote.

"You can come back tomorrow. We open at 6 A.M. daily. You sure everything is all right?"

"Yes, I'm fine, thank you. I just fell asleep admiring the wonderful stained glass."

"Lots of folk come to see those windows. I must admit,

I'm rather partial to them myself. You just come back next time, okay? My name is Charles. I'm always here."

"Thank you Charles. I'm Mariel. By the way Charles, did you see the little girl who came in here before? She raced in like she owned the place and disappeared behind that niche right there," Mariel pointed out.

"Child? No, can't say that I did. Today's been so quiet, I didn't even know you were here. There's nothing behind that niche, ma'am. Maybe you were already sleeping...," he said with a gentle chuckle.

"Oh, it's all right, Charles. Maybe I was," Mariel mused with a knowing smile on her face. "I'm so glad that I met you, and you can be sure I'll be back again. This place will always be very special to me."

As the huge church doors closed behind her concealing the humble parting smile from Charles, Mariel felt thoroughly renewed. While her meeting with Sebastian had been interrupted, its meaning was forever preserved. He *was* near. Everything was real. She could paint now!

Chapter Sixteen

Transformation

The next week was a blur of activity. After dutifully restocking her refrigerator and pantry, Mariel placed her phone in the silent mode and dove right into painting. In a few days she had completed the cobalt collection, the moonstone collection, and had sketched a huge mural of the buttercup and liquid citrine-ribboned highway from a much earlier memory. Never had she felt more alive and productive. The brushes obeyed her vision impeccably. She felt Sebastian very near. One more week would probably do it. She couldn't remember being happier.

She was awakened from her reverie by a familiar voice. Celeste was insistently pounding on the door.

"Mari, are you in there? Mari, please open.... I came straight from the airport and don't have the key. We're worried sick about you. Mari...."

"Why all the ruckus?" Mariel challenged as she threw open the door to welcome her dear friend.

"*Ruckus?* You had us *frantic*, Mari! " chided Celeste as she threw her arms around Mariel.

"Your mom hadn't heard from you. You didn't answer

my calls. I've been gone for two weeks now— since I met the man of my dreams—and you ask *why the ruckus?* Look at you— covered head to toe with paint. Whew! Let's open some windows here. Whoa, Mari...this is amazing. You *have* been busy, girlfriend!"

Celeste stood in rapt wonder at the looming canvasses. Never would she have even imagined such compelling beauty and amazing color. Hardly able to catch her breath, she stood mesmerized.

"Mari... this is absolutely unbelieveable! I've never seen anything like this in my life. Mari...you are...this is a miracle!"

"You could say that again. It's almost as if I am witnessing the paint flow out of my brushes and onto the canvasses. It takes me back... you know...to the realm and the children... and Sebastian. I can't tell you the feeling I have now that it's really on canvas. The faces in my memories seem to emerge from the colors. Their eyes, their smiles, their purity and beauty... these children want the world to know how good and kindly is the one who brought them to safety. Violence does not have the last word."

"Mari, this will blow the locks off the minds of the whole world. I can't even believe what I'm seeing. How could you do this in just two weeks?" Celeste had breathlessly collapsed on the paint spattered couch, still clutching the champagne bottle she had in hand.

"Actually, Cel, it was *one* week. I got into a creative slump for a week. I was tormented by doubt and darkness. I couldn't get past the sketches to bring the babies to life. It was awful."

"You're telling me that you spent a week in torment, and then painted all of this in seven days?"

"It's true. I can't believe it myself. In fact, except for the joy of seeing you safe and sound, I'd be painting right now. It is miraculous in a way. But, what's with the champagne, and what was that about the love of your life? ," Mariel teased as she tried to turn her attention to her dear friend. She needed a breather and this was the perfect segue.

"Mari, anything I was about to say or celebrate has been cosmically dwarfed by this exhibition! Do you realize what you have here? Do you have *any* idea how these panels just steal all breath away and whisk you to another world? Just like you to try to change the subject. Mari, you are amazing. This is a gift—your gift to the world and I'm absolutely blown away! We have to call your mother. She was assuring me that you were probably just busy, trying to convince herself, you know, but first: She has to know you're okay, second: She has to see these!"

"Okay, Celeste, take a breath! Thanks. I'm glad you like them. I'm pretty okay with the way they turned out so far. It's almost as if they emerge— once I start painting. Everything comes back in vivid detail, and it's like I'm there again. It's humbling really. Yeah, I guess I need to call mom, and will but—champagne? You know me, I don't drink more than a glass and still have the bottle we opened *before* you left. I'm sensing something very exciting...sit down and tell me!"

"Mari, I guess this has been a magical week for both of us. His name is Greg Marceau, and you've got to meet him! Forget old champagne. Knowing you, it has probably gone flat. I'll have to get you one of those stoppers that keep the bubbles. Anyway… this trip turned out to be the most exciting surprise ever!"

The champagne was poured, and Celeste described her encounter with this wonderful Greg whom she continued to see for the week following the wedding. Mariel absorbed her friend's happiness like the bubbling libation, and listened attentively to every detail.

"Celeste, he sounds great! So when do I get to meet him?"

"Well, he wanted to come this weekend, but I put him off. It was all such a whirlwind, I thought I needed some space. Could it be real? And then there's work. I have to catch up or I'll lose my job. So he won't come until next month. He texts me all the time, and we video chat. Come on, let's get on right now. I want to show him your work."

"Slow down Celeste. Not yet. *No one* is to see these canvasses until the event. I'm sworn to secrecy. Besides, look at me—he'd think you were crazy to have a paint speckled artist friend like me. In time, Cellie. First, and foremost, I've got to finish the series. Steve Irving wants a sampling to go to the graphics department in two weeks for a calendar and posters. *He* hasn't even seen these yet, and I did sign an exclusive. You're the only one, and you can't breathe a word to anyone…swear, okay?"

"Don't worry, Mari. Your secrets have always been safe with me, as you know. Listen, it's late, and I'm really zonked. Would you mind if I crashed out right here tonight? I'll make you breakfast in the morning and be on my way so that you can finish. Okay, sis?"

"Of course, I'd love that if you can stand the mess! I have an air mattress in the hall closet you'll love. Shower, or run a bath, and I'll have it set up for you in short order. I hope you don't mind, but I plan to do a little more painting before I close my eyes."

"Not even the war of the worlds could keep me up tonight. I think I finally ran out of adrenaline after two weeks. This will be sweet. Actually, that bath idea sounds great. I've always admired your discernment of bath fragrance and candle essences. That would be just the place for my last glass of champagne. Mari, it's great seeing you on a roll again. A final toast— friends forever!"

And with the tinkling of champagne flutes, Celeste was off to her bath as Mari arranged a comfortable bed for her in the half loft up above the studio. The skylight showered down the soft radiance of a full moon as she looked up wistfully. Stars like moonstones... she thought, and each one has a story...."

Chapter Seventeen

Morning

"Rise and shine, sunshine ! We both slept in, and it's 10 A.M. Here's your coffee just the way you like it, and I've got some scones in the oven. How do you like your eggs?"

Rubbing the sleep from her paint sprayed eyes and face, Mari was happy to awaken to her best friend's company. She had painted for a few hours longer after setting up the mattress and had hardly noticed when Celeste finally mounted the short spiral stairway to the loft saying her goodnight.

The light amber tones of the champagne had set her mood to bringing to life the buttercup covered meadows and aerial highway of lighted ribbons. She converted the sketch into vibrant living color and dimension—or at least a portion of it. This was to be a huge mural from which the haunting eyes of her dark period—recessed but present— were overwhelmed by the joyous light and warmth of the golden tones, and finally orange and copper flames of light which spread in a forceful crescendo to a rapturous explosion. Staring at her work as she sipped the coffee,

Mari began this day feeling wonderfully alive and grateful. Her vision was becoming a reality. *Their* children would speak to the world. Sebastian was near, and she couldn't wait to finish this mural!

After a hearty breakfast and the overwhelming admiration of her dear friend, Mariel once again focused in on her world of gem babies. As she played Barber's *Adagio for Strings*, Vaughan Williams' *Lark Ascending* and others of her favorite orchestral pieces, she couldn't help but notice how none approached the beauty and layered harmonies of the realm. If only those could be reproduced, she thought!

It was well into the evening when Mariel realized that she hadn't stopped since locking the door after Celeste left. She had just about finished the mural, and rested back in humble appreciation for how the faces and facets had flowed out onto the canvasses as if new life was entering this world! That is exactly what it all meant! Only she and Sebastian really knew this feeling. How intimately this creative process had woven them together. That is what sustained her as she painted hour after hour. Those creative hours were times spent with Sebastian feeling very near.

Tonight she would relax and clean up with a fragrant and bubbling bath. She had reached her goal. Only the original red scene and the pearly opalescent cave scene remained. In a few days she would have those completed and ready for Steve to see first, and then the graphic artists to design the promotional posters and calendars. The exhibition would be held in New York in the large loggia of the Metropolitan Museum of Art, exclusively reserved for this rollout on behalf of the ICC and its counterparts.

Celebrities were endorsing the work in large numbers and would be present with the major media outlets racing for exclusive interviews. Mariel was booked from morning to night for the week following the exhibition on all the major talk shows from *Good Morning America* to the late shows. Somehow she'd get through all that, but thankfully for now, all she had to do was paint.

Steve wanted a self portrait, and she had decided to do it after the other panels were done. She could see it in her mind's eye, and more than anything looked forward to completing it. For now she was so relaxed and content that she fell asleep immediately. The next thing she knew she was awakened by the phone ringing. Celeste must have taken the phone off the mute setting before she left.

"That little sneak…," she thought as she opened the shades on a gloriously bright and cheerful morning.

"Mariel, Steve Irving, here. How is everything going? When can I come to see what you have?"

"Oh, hi Steve—good to hear from you. Everything is going quite well. I should have the entire exhibition ready for you by Friday. I'd prefer that you see the canvasses in daylight, however, so how does Saturday sound?"

"Great, Mariel. Hold on while I have Suzanne check the flights." As she waited she scanned the studio. Aside from the amazing canvasses, the place was a shambles. She'd have to get it cleaned up before presenting her work to Steve. Maybe she could just pay someone to do it.

Her thoughts were soon interrupted by Steve's assertive voice again.

"Mariel, I'll get into Logan around 10:30 A.M. on

Saturday and will catch a cab. How long do you think it will take me to get to your place, under an hour?"

"Without a doubt Steve, especially on Saturday morning. I'll expect you before noon. How long will you be staying?"

"Oh, I'll just fly up for the day. Pick a really nice restaurant—you know, Boston's finest, and I'll take you out to lunch to celebrate after I've seen your work. Suzanne has me booked on a 6:50 P.M. flight out of Logan so I'll beat it right back here. That should be enough time, don't you think?"

"It should work if that's what you had in mind."

"Oh, one more thing, Mariel. Please compose a few ideas for a self portrait. We'd like to use that for the press releases, without leaking the actual exhibition pieces ahead of time. See you on Saturday, then!"

"Fine, Steve. Thanks for the call and see you then."

"Whew! I owe you one, Cellie! It's a good thing I didn't miss *that* call," thought Mariel as she threw cold water on her face and started the coffee.

It was Sunday and all was well with the world. She intended to add the final touches to the buttercup mural and bring the pearl cave sketch into living color. That would leave the original red gem baby, which she had decided would be a close-up of the faceted chunk of gem with the original demure face peering out. Two days on each would be fine as long as she had no interruptions. That would leave Thursday and Friday for touch ups and finishes, and yes, getting the apartment *and herself*, cleaned up.

Chapter Eighteen

Labor of love

As Mariel awoke on Thursday morning, she was comforted by her accomplishments and how she had finished more quickly than she had thought possible. Except for the self-portrait, she was done. What an amazing life odyssey she was journaling here, and only her mother and Celeste knew the back story. Of course, Sebastian was part of it and knew of it, but it was their intimate story. Now, she felt a swell of excitement rise in her as she anticipated unveiling the entire collection to Steve in just two days! With all the rest just drying on this wonderfully bright morning, Mariel couldn't wait to start the self portrait!

She had it all planned out. She would be standing in front of a large canvas, paintbrush in hand. The canvas in front of her would be in its early stages, not too delineated but sketchy, with washy tones laying out the subject of a gem baby. The under painting and sketch would be in sienna, and subdued. She would be wearing rich, sapphire blue jeans and a turquoise big shirt, with her thick wavy auburn tresses casually whisked up and off her neck with a tortoise shell clasp. On her left shoulder would be a bright yellow finch, and while she had the paintbrush in her right hand, she would have her head tilted toward her left shoulder as if listening to the bird. Sebastian would be there, ready to whisper in her left ear, with his two hands gently clutching both of her upper arms as if he didn't want to startle her. Sebastian would be muted in colors, and slightly ethereal.

"Like a bird whispering in your ear...," she painfully recalled.

With a sigh from the depths of her soul she exhaled, and with a new breath jumped into painting overdrive. It was her way to be connected with Sebastian. She could see the whole painting in her mind's eye and needed only to transfer it onto the canvas. As she painted, she sensed that she was *uncovering* it more than painting it. Once again she experienced a kind of birthing as she feverishly painted and studied how each stroke seemed to breathe life into yet another panel which emerged with a life of its own. Mariel was witnessing the miracle of her creative gift in humble awe of its latest manifestation.

The next thing she knew it was midnight. She realized that her eyes were burning, and that she was terribly thirsty and thoroughly exhausted. She was done for now. The rest would be finessed tomorrow, or rather, later on today, Friday. She stepped back and smiled. The canvas almost breathed, just the way she hoped it would. After a tall glass of water and brushing her teeth, she slumped onto the couch and fell immediately and contentedly to sleep.

Fresh Air

Awakened by the bright morning sun, Mariel jumped out of her bed with exhilaration. She went immediately to the windows and opened them all to freshen the place and add to the drying of the canvasses. She picked up her phone as she walked over to the coffee pot.

"Good Morning Cellie, time to smell the coffee, girlfriend. I need your support and help."

"Wow Mar, this is way early for you… and me. What time is it anyway? Did you say that you needed, help?" Celeste yawned and stretched in an effort to gather herself.

"Here's the scoop, Cell. Steve will be here before noon tomorrow to see *everything* I've got. If he thinks it's ready, there will be a photo shoot here, or else in New York after everything is crated up and trucked there in the next week few weeks. Are you with me, Cell? Okay. First, you know it looked like we had color blizzard in here. Granted the drop cloths got most of it, but I think I'm going to let all the furniture go and pretend this is just a studio. I can sleep on the air mattress in the loft, anyway. But who can I call to clean up this place and move the furniture out? I'll pay them whatever it takes. It's just that I'm clueless."

"Uh… give me a sec here, Mari. I was in Fiji or something in my dreams when you called and now you need immediate answers. Okay sis, I've got this. But, is that it? It sounded like you were just starting a list. Is there more?"

"Just one little thing, Cellie. I want you here when Steve comes. Please. He's a bit overwhelming, and I'm nervous enough already. Please, Cell. I'll make it up to you and owe you big time for a month, but you've got to say yes. Cel...?"

"Well, I don't know Mariel...I had plans to take my yacht over to Hyannis tomorrow, but I guess I just might be able to reschedule," Celeste quipped wryly. "Of *course* I will, Mariel! You know the only yacht I have is an origami one. There is nothing in the world I'd *rather* do than meet someone as important as Steve Irving and watch as he drools over your work! Now, about cleaning up the place... give me a half an hour and I'll have a plan. Talk to you soon!"

Sure enough, Celeste had contracted a group of college students intent on making some extra money, to move the furniture to the Good Hunting Thrift Store. Then, she sent her building super's relatives to clean. They were always looking for a little extra income so this was a mutual benefit. By lunch time the place was sparkling, airy and the perfect showcase for Mariel's panels. Mariel thanked Lucia profusely and packed her up with last year's spring and winter coats, and some sweaters as well as a generous check. She called Celeste and headed out to meet her for lunch.

Gearing Up

"Okay Mar, what's the game plan? Tell me about Steve, and what you want me to say or do when he comes," said Celeste excitedly.

They were enjoying salads and soup in good spirits as they looked forward to this long awaited day, but Mariel, always unaffected, felt no need for a game plan.

"Steve is a driver, or bulldozer, to be more accurate. There is no need for me to do anything but be ready for him to call the shots. He's flying in around 10:30 and will take a cab. That puts him on the hill about 11:30, or 11:45 if he checked any baggage, which I doubt. We meet and greet, he sees my work, we go out to lunch to discuss the details, and hopefully celebrate. I want you with me, Celeste, for lunch too. I'm afraid I'll be so overwhelmed by him I might not even remember what he says. Anyway, I've made reservations at J. Downey's for 1:15 in case he wants to walk there. Otherwise, we'll take a cab. I don't want him even seeing your rusty 96 Volvo, so don't offer," Mari said with a wink.

"Talk about 'puttin' on the ritz,' I'll say... J. Downey's, woo hoo! The only thing I've tasted there would be their mint flavored toothpicks which I sampled as I salivated over the menu, and then gagged on the prices. Who picked the place?"

"Steve said to pick the best place in town, and so I did. He flies back out at 6:50, so he'll be wanting a cab around 4, I guess. Can you believe it, Cellie...? This day has finally come."

"What a life!"

"Yes, life..." she replied with tears of joy and sadness both competing.

Chapter Nineteen

The Unveiling

When the downstairs bell sounded, Mariel and Celeste froze in an excited and terrified stare before leaping to the intercom to buzz him in.

"It's me, Mariel, you can let me in," came the signature bellowing that could only be Steve's.

"Great Steve, take the elevator to the top, and we'll be there to show you in."

"Hello, hello, hello, good to see you, Mariel," Steve boomed with a quick embrace and kiss on the cheek as he bounded off the elevator. I must say, it's great to be in Bean Town again. You've picked the best location here on Beacon Hill for a view! Oh, and who do we have here?"

"Steve, I'd like you to meet my very best friend, Celeste Martini."

With a gallant bow and a warm handshake, he had Celeste swooning immediately.

"Well, with a last name like that, I think we share a common interest already! Pleased to meet you, Celeste."

"I've heard so much about you and your work Steve;

truly the honor is mine. I think you'll find Mari's work is truly amazing," Celeste managed to stutter awkwardly.

"I'm glad the wait is *finally* over. Shall we then? " he offered energetically as he glanced down the hall wondering which door would open to her studio and reveal the new collection.

"Before we enter, Steve, I'd rather that my paintings speak for themselves so I won't be adding any commentary. Just allow them to take you in, and we'll talk later. Agreed?" Mariel ventured with surprising confidence.

"By all means, I can respect that."

As Mariel opened the sunlit studio with the sheer drapery panels gently billowing in the mild breeze at the tall, open windows, Steve was immediately and completely astonished. It was not just the amazing, other-worldly use of color for these extraordinary scenes, but the immediacy of the life-like faces that seemed to pulse out of the canvasses as if they were actually breathing. He slowly spun around as if dazed and in a trance, viewing the panels all around him. He felt as if the faces were speaking personally to him, and having seen them, he knew he could never forget them or the stories they had to tell of thousands of forgotten and voiceless innocents. Speech was impossible as he looked into their gentle yet piercing eyes sparkling through a myriad of shimmering faceted jewels. He almost thought that he heard music and water, as he slowly paused from face to face. He was completely overwhelmed by the power and beauty of this world Mariel had created.

After about twenty minutes of absolute silence, he dryly and weakly asked for a chair, which he sank into as if completely drained.

"Steve, would you like some water or coffee?"

"Water would be great, Mariel. Thank you," he nearly whispered.

Mariel didn't expect this reaction and found herself very unprepared for it. Celeste, too, was beside herself. She almost thought that Steve was going to cry.

"Is everything all right, Steve? Are you okay? ," Mariel inquired with deep empathy.

"Mariel, if I had not seen these with my own eyes, I would not have believed it. Never in my life have I been so overtaken by the power of beauty and innocence, of pathos and tragedy, of peace and triumph, of entreaty and inspiration all at the same time! Never! I have been to the Louvre, the Vatican, Prado, Tate—you name every great museum of the world, and I have been there more than once. I am a life-long purveyor and collector of fine art, but never has anything moved me in the way that your canvasses have. Mariel, they *breathed*!

I thought they were 3D with a soundtrack! I heard a thousand voices singing, and water tumbling and flowing, and those eyes...Mariel...the eyes! Never did I expect anything like this! You have so far exceeded my expectations that I humbly beg your forgiveness at offering you so little. Mariel, what you have done is monumental and will serve our cause like a powerful wind in our waiting sails. It's precisely what we needed, but much more! This will not only take the art world by storm, but the public as well, and the exploited, abused, and trafficked citizens of the world will at last be known to everyone. No one can see these and not be moved and challenged. Mariel, I had no idea you were such a force! I'm truly humbled and grateful...."

"Steve, I hardly know what to say. I have never seen you like this, and I was worried that you were somehow disappointed."

"Disappointed? Hell no! I was in pain, actually! But it was the pain of beholding such unspeakable beauty, which the heart and mind know they cannot process, but only surrender to. It is the kind of beauty that could slay a dragon with merely a nod, or quiet a tornado with the touch of a feather. It is completely disarming. These speak a language only our deepest soul understands and longs for, where goodness and right make sense and reign supreme. It is the kind of beauty that puts a seed in your soul that you feel take root and grow so that you want to sing and dance and shout a thousand times: YES! YES! To truth, goodness and beauty—forever! Mariel, you've done it, my girl," he trumpeted as he lifted her in his arms and tightly swung her around as if dancing with a child in his embrace.

A bit dizzy and completely taken by surprise Mariel stammered breathlessly,

"Wow, Steve, I'm glad you feel so strongly about them. I didn't realize how much they affected you," she continued as he gently landed her on her feet while balancing her with one hand until she was steady.

"Whew! Sorry if I took you by surprise there. These paintings completely swept me away, so I had to return the favor, Mariel. I can't believe you painted all of these here in this rather small studio! You are an amazing artist."

"Yes, I painted them all right here. You still haven't seen

the self-portrait, though. It's behind the Cove of Lights panel."

"Do you mean to tell me that you painted that too? I was hoping for a few sketches, and thought I might have been pushing it to expect that," he said as he jumped to his feet like an eager pup.

"Oh, Mariel, this is breathtaking. How tender and intimate...," he said after a few minutes of meditative absorption. "I can see the deep love between you and Sebastian... and what a nice touch with the yellow finch. Do you mind if I ask if that has a special meaning?"

"I rather expected that, but I'd prefer not to go into it at this point," Mariel returned pensively.

Steve understood. With a clap, he swung around and changed the topic: "Did you make those lunch reservations? I feel as if I've been through a four act play here and need some refueling! How about you *and* Celeste? I hope you'll join us too? , " he boomed as he once more commanded his usual vigor and decisiveness.

"Sure Steve. It's all set and they're expecting us at 1:15. J. Downey's is a fifteen minute walk from here or we can call a cab," Muriel submitted.

"If you girls are up for it, let's walk! I'd love to breathe in and feel the air of good old Boston—getting some exercise while I'm at it. After all, it's back on the plane right after this. What a great day this has turned out to be! Mariel, you've made me a very happy man!"

Mariel and Celeste looked at each other with a sigh of relief and excitement while riding on his enthusiasm which could carry a whole city in its wake.

It was amid the savory flavors of good food and strong coffee that Steve settled down to talk business.

"Mariel, how soon will the paintings be dry enough to crate up and transport to New York?"

"I think about two weeks would do it, to play safe."

"Here's what's going to happen then. On Monday I'll call my graphics team and send them down to shoot the collection for the calendar and posters. I'll also send an insurance man so that the whole shebang is insured. Once they have the photos, they can start the posters and brochures—advertising that is—while they work on commemorative prints for purchase at the event and beyond. Then, on the 28th, I'll send in the team to crate it all up and put it on the truck for New York. You, my dear, are getting a $10,000 bonus. Go to a spa—pretty up, get a dress and whatever you'd like. This is black tie, so glam up like it's the Oscars. I'll arrange the hotel accommodations for you right near the Metropolitan, and air travel, of course. You'll probably want a few new things for T.V. interviews, etc. The $10,000 is for you *personally*. Mariel you are a paintbrush warrior, and I know this was a lot of work. I knew you were good, but you have proved yourself to be great. I insist—take my check and get ready for the red carpet. It's a lot of fuss I know, but do it for the kids. Our culture feeds off celebrity, and you my dear, are about to be launched!"

"Steve, I couldn't...that is far too much, I can't accept...."

"Nonsense! You must! This is part of it, and really for things like this it's expected, and hardly extravagant. You are our most important advertisement and you need to be at your absolute best. You're already a natural beauty, but you know, get a facial, or whatever women do at the spa. It will relax you for the high intensity to follow. And, if I might suggest a dress the color of your ring, I think that would be truly stunning, but just a suggestion…it's entirely up to you."

Almost there

The following weeks were wild with activity and meetings over media releases, scripts for interviews, photo shoots and more. After the panels were crated and shipped off, Mariel looked at her bare studio and drew a deep breath. She felt naked and alone without the company of her gem babies and the powerful reminders of Sebastian. In a week she'd be in New York for the public unveiling and gala. Suddenly she felt fragile and alone. Thankfully, she had a week to go shopping and to a spa and more than enough money to do both. She insisted that Celeste accompany her, not only for shopping and a spa day, but also to the gala.

As soon as she laid eyes on the gown, she knew it was perfect. Cobalt blue satin with peacock feather embroidery wisping down the left shoulder and diagonally across the bodice and waist to the opposite hip, with a full length skirt which flared below the knees—seemed made just for her! She'd get earrings to match her stunning ring and weave a peacock feather behind each ear into her full, wavy hair. Perhaps a silver shawl and clutch would set it off without her needing a necklace of any kind. Celeste concurred. She looked elegant and glamorous, but not overstated—just the way she had hoped. Celeste chose a mint green, fitted gown, complete with a large, coral colored satin flower and bow tied at the waist, and a chiffon shawl. She had her hair up, with a matching satin flower. With her olive skin tone, she too was a picture of feminine youth and beauty.

Chapter Twenty

Showtime

The evening of the much anticipated and slightly dreaded gala had come. Steve had his limo arrive for Mariel and Celeste at the hotel. As Mariel approached the limo Steve jumped out to give her a kiss on the cheek, and was totally overcome by how beautiful she looked.

"Mariel... you are *more* than stunning! I don't know which is more beautiful—you or your paintings. And Celeste dear, aren't *you* lovely? I feel like the proud father of the two of you, but I have William from the Center here to escort you for the evening, Celeste. I'll need to keep Mariel near."

"...and from fainting, Steve. I don't know if I'm up for the spotlight. I love painting, but have grown rather private since Sebastian left. If only the evening and this week were already over."

"Now, now, dear one—**none** of that. There isn't a celebrity here who can outshine you tonight. With your beauty and talent, you will undoubtedly catch the eye of every available bachelor in the world by evening's end and...."

Mariel interrupted emphatically.

"Steve. Allow me to make one thing clear at the gate. I'll never love anyone but Sebastian. I'm not interested in bachelors. Even though I know that you mean well, frankly, the whole idea is—well, abhorrent."

"*Abhorrent,* Mariel, is a very strong word," Steve submitted.

"...for the strongest of feelings Steve. Is that clear? Please don't allow anyone to entertain any hopes in my regard—ever. Please promise me that much, and please understand that I do appreciate your concern."

"Banish the gloom, and cheer up, Mariel. This is a celebration, and yes, I will abide by your wishes. With you on my paternal arm all evening, you'll be protected. Don't worry. Consider me your guardian. Your mother arrived, right?"

"Yes, she texted that she was seated just a little while ago, and thanks Steve...for understanding how I feel."

"Now are you ready for the podium? I looked over your acknowledgement remarks, and brief and elegant as they are, I think they're fine. We'll let the work speak for itself, as you suggested to me when I saw your canvasses firsthand. I'll introduce you, and one of the underwriters will bring you to the podium. After the accolades and presentation of flowers, you'll have the mike. Just when you'll have all eyes completely enraptured, we'll pull the drapes off each panel and invite the dignitaries first, then everyone else, to walk through the loggia. There will be a quartet and harpist playing. Champagne and cocktails as well as finger food will be served while all linger and bid on the silent auction. Seating for the dinner will start at 7 PM, when we'll present the work and future goals of Invisible Crimes Centers with a new promo film. Your entire collection will be featured throughout as the new logo and mascot of our work. The mayor as well as the museum curator will have their say, and then we'll have dessert and start awarding the silent auction items. (I'm bidding on the Fiji trip for you and a friend—and if you don't win—I'll *send* you there after the media blitz week is over.) Oh, they will be purchasing the coffee table book of this collection, as well as posters and calendars. Did I tell you the *Times* will feature you in the Arts and Leisure section of the Sunday paper? That's big, Mariel! And that is only the beginning! Mariel, they are going to love you! You'll see...." he reassured with a side hug.

"I wish I could be as excited as you, Steve. I feel weak... and wish I were invisible, frankly."

"Here, Mariel, a toast!" as he handed her a tall flute of champagne. Have a sip of this with some sushi and you'll be fine. I will stand near after introducing you, if you like," he said with his hand gently lifting her chin to look into his caring and fatherly eyes.

"Please do, Steve. I'd appreciate that. I'll pass on the champagne though, and honestly couldn't think of eating anything."

Thunderous applause and a standing ovation greeted Mariel. As she glanced around waiting for the accolades to subside, she thought of Sebastian with whom she shared this recognition. Everyone knew of his work and his tragic death. Suddenly, as if out of nowhere, there was a distracted buzz filtering through the crowd. Mariel didn't understand until she felt a light wisp of air and something like a feather tickle her shoulder. She felt the timid bird and heard the gentle chirping near her ear. It seemed unafraid as she tilted her head toward her left shoulder.

It was a yellow finch! Now a confident smile rushed over her—along with a flush of excitement—as she thought of her beloved Sebastian.

Photographers started snapping wildly, and as Mariel held her hand up to keep the delicate bird from being frightened, she looked at her sapphire ring. Was it her imagination, or did she see Sebastian smiling from ear to ear reflected in it? She recalled his words about the ring: "…you'll see in a while." And of course, the bird! He was here—near as he promised! She felt his presence and breathed in a new confidence and composure.

Finally the crowd settled down as the curator, Rudy, who was a friend of Steve's, came to stage. He explained that the latch had come loose from the aviary he sheltered down the hall, overlooking the patio. Luckily it was discovered as soon as it happened but not soon enough to prevent one of the birds from escaping. *Sunny*, as he referred to the bold and bright finch—was very used to him since this aviary was like a garden through which he walked and even fed some of the birds out of his hand. He marveled at how amazing this particular escape was, given the fact that while it had not been planned, Mariel had, in fact, chosen to include a bright yellow finch in her self-portrait.

Wild applause ensued once more as Mariel approached the mike with great stature and assurance. Amazingly, Sunny stayed put.

"Thank you all very much. It has been my pleasure to offer my paintings for this, a cause particularly dear to my heart ever since I was a little girl. My mom is here tonight, and she can attest that the gem babies have captivated me since that time. She understands the depth of their meaning and has always encouraged me to "tell their story," as it were. Thanks, mom! As for this evening, the support and warm appreciation you have all shown for this project... I would like to say that I accept it not only on my behalf, but especially on behalf of my beloved and departed husband—Sebastian Turner."

As she turned toward the bird on her shoulder again, she could feel it ever so gently nibbling on her ear. Her heart was about to explode with joy. When the spontaneous applause had subsided she continued:

"But rather than words, I would like to offer you my paintings. I can only hope that they will speak to you and many others and move your hearts to champion and support ICC on behalf of countless invisible victims of violence and abuse. Thank you."

The curator came with a millet treat to woo Sunny off her shoulder. Steve jumped up to the mike to announce the revealing of her breathtaking panels and took her arm to escort her off the stage. Along the walls of the loggia, large graceful draperies concealed the treasured collection until now. With a pull on the elegant roping, the suited and gloved ushers simultaneously parted the drapes and seventeen different panels were revealed. A collective "ah" resonated through the loggia as the colors and faces of the *gem babies* began to work their magic on the crowd. Statesmen and women, movie celebs, artists, writers, journalists and media reps, social workers, donors and invited guests of every profession were taken in as if absorbed by the appealing drama of hope and goodness over violence and despair represented in each face.

Artist Credit: Marguerite La Roche

"Mariel, you were wonderful, just wonderful!" Steve hugged her with warm exuberance and kept her near. He leaned in to whisper in her ear. "I have some exciting news. While I can't know for certain how much this will mean, I still have to share the latest with you regarding the recovery of Sebastian's work. Remember my connection in Grozny, the one I call Gordon? Not his real name by the way. Well, he got a flash drive out of Chechnya through a diplomatic pouch which arrived at the Embassy in D.C. with instructions to deliver it to me. A courier will bring it tomorrow. This is highly classified and protected, and Mariel, it could be the breakthrough we've been waiting for! We *might* have some files recovered from Sebastian's computer and *possibly*, just possibly—some with his latest findings. Remember, the operative words are *"might"* and *"possibly."* I don't want this crushing you if we discover nothing new. Most importantly, not a single word of this to the press, however, or our contacts in Grozny would be compromised, possibly even killed. What a day! Before noon tomorrow, we should have the drive. Now, let's mingle and eavesdrop on some of the reactions to your work. Here's some champagne. Are you up for it?"

Her confidence was not only restored, but infused with a kind of dauntless vigor. In anticipation of what she might learn in less than twelve hours, she was up for anything! She glanced at her ring again, hoping to catch a loving glance from Sebastian. It was there! He *was* with her. He was sharing and drinking in the wonders of this night and toasting what this would mean in sparing the vulnerable, as well as apprehending the perpetrators. She did not feel alone, and in fact—exuded the glowing assurance of a beneficent queen who had won the affection and admiration of all her subjects and the undying loyalty of her court and would reign happily for years to come.

If this sounded like a fairy tale, that night most certainly seemed like one. As she recalled it in all its beauty and marvel, though some decades later—it still filled her heart with wonder and awe. This was the back story which until now only her mother and Celeste (and of course dear Sebastian) knew.

Chapter Twenty-One

The euphoria from the evening gala lingered into the morning. To top that off, today was the day she might learn more about dear Sebastian's work. Steve had insisted that she meet him for brunch in his office. Coffee, croissants with ham and cheese were ready and waiting when she arrived at 9:30 A.M. Mariel was breathless with anticipation as she burst through the doors of his office.

"Did it arrive yet?"

"Not yet, Mari—sit down and have some coffee. Let's talk about this, Mari. For all we know this could be old information, or, somehow compromised. Gordon told me that a mole had worked with some of Vorona's men and had seen firsthand some of the holding sites for girls who had been lured into this grotesque trade under the pretext of job placement."

"Who is Vorona?"

"Vorona—is the bad guy—originally from Moscow. He set up shop in Chechnya because of the instability there and the inability of any one side to prosecute under the present unrest. Furthermore, the desperation in the area led orphaned girls to prostitution and made them easy targets of human traffickers. His name in Russian means "crow," and his heart is as black as coal. We suspect that his lucrative trafficking business is really a means for buying arms that fuel the factional infighting between Chechnya and Georgia right now. You're not eating, Mari. Have a croissant."

"Thanks Steve, maybe after we receive the package. My stomach is completely tied up in knots right now. Do you think this could lead us to Sebastian's murderers?"

"To be honest, that is expecting too much. However, any information helps. We already know that Vorona is the main operative in Chechnya. He doesn't tolerate rivals and heads the drug as well as prostitution and trafficking trades in Grozny. He gets the girls as well as boys addicted so that they will do anything for their coke or heroine, and—well—you get the picture. The problem is that all of the police are on the take since they fear for their families. Looking the other way guarantees their own families will be untouched, and even moved out of Chechnya for safety and of course, immunity. Until the government stabilizes, the brutes rule alongside the military factions who have strong-armed the opposition. The people are scared and powerless."

"...just the kind of situation that crime thrives on, as well as dictatorship."

"Exactly. It's actually amazing that Sebastian lasted as long as he did. Any foreign journalists are viewed as targets since this group thrives on obscurity and the kind of silence that comes from terror. It was his prowess with Russian that gave him an edge."

As Mariel drifted off thinking of her dear Sebastian, she remembered the long nights he studied Russian during college. He was not content to read Dostoevsky or Solzhenitsyn in English. It had to be in Russian. When his journalism led him to that part of the world, he immersed himself in the language and culture so as to move freely. His passion for it propelled his assimilation. In a few years he was reading and writing Russian very convincingly.

Just then, the receptionist buzzed Steve. There was a courier with a package he needed to sign off on.

"It's here, Mari. Hang on and I'll be right back!"

In a few moments he was tearing at the brown paper package. Inside was one flash drive, with a Russian inscription hand-written on a tag, which dangled from it. He immediately put it on his laptop so that they could see its contents.

"Darn! The whole thing is in Russian! I didn't see that coming! However, there is a web translator we could use. I'm just not sure how safe it is to do that here. I think we ought to go down to the State Department or Pentagon or something."

"Ugh...to get so close and have to wait is hard—but I guess you're right. If we've waited this long, we should do it right. I imagine that the Pentagon or State Department has secure translation software we could use. Perhaps we should check first. But Steve, what about the interviews?"

"Of course, you'll have to keep them, but not a word to them about this Mari. Let me have Suzanne call Senator Borgen. He'll know who we should see. He and I went to high school and did our undergraduate studies together at N.Y.U. You're up for a trip to Washington in a week or so, right? That will give you time to complete your appearances and promote the exhibit. Oh, I'll take care of the expenses, so don't worry about that. What do you say, Mari? " he rambled, dunking croissant after croissant into his coffee and gulping them down with great satisfaction.

"Steve, there is nothing more important to me than following whatever crumbs we might find from Sebastian's trail. Whatever it takes, I'm in!"

The Senator agreed that the information should be read and documented in a secure setting. Once the intelligence community was involved, it was decided that Langley was the best place. The earliest meeting time would be next Thursday, eight days away since the senator would be out of state for the week and Steve didn't want anyone else intervening for now. Borgen would have his driver pick Steve and Mariel up at the hotel in D.C. and together they'd drive to the auspicious headquarters of the CIA in Langley, Virginia.

In his usual protective and gracious manner Steve insisted that Mariel take time off in between interviews, most of which were taped in the early morning, to enjoy the art treasures of New York City. Her mother was taking a nurses' training course back in Boston and had flown out early the day after the gala. Except for Steve and Rudy, Mariel was alone, since Celeste, too, had returned to Boston. This interval would allow her to visit museums, catch some shows and concerts, *and relax*, he said. As always, he put her up in grand style, sparing no expense. They would leave next Wednesday. He also insisted on dinner out each evening when he returned from his ICC office, and surprised her with Broadway tickets for Friday.

Chapter Twenty-Two

A Crushing Blow

Having the opportunity to visit the Metropolitan Museum of Art again was like breathing *rainbows* instead of air for Mariel! Coinciding with the exhibit of her collection was a gem exhibit! She never tired of staring at gems and allowing them to take her back to those magical *gem babies*. She felt that she could always improve her ability to capture the way light and facet played on one another in their lively duets. She called Rudy, the curator who was going to allow her some private viewing time, and have lunch with her.

As Mariel made her way to the loggia, she was surprised by the cordons which designated the area as off limits. When Rudy came out to meet her and allow her passage, he looked drawn and downcast.

"What's wrong Rudy? You seemed so excited on the phone yesterday. You said that the collection was drawing more people every day. What is going on?"

"Oh Mariel, excuse me. It has nothing to do with you. Well, almost nothing. It's Sunny. I should have named him Houdini. He managed another escape, and well, it was his last..." Rudy turned to hide the tears that were welling up.

Gasping with surprise Mariel couldn't imagine how Sunny could get out of this colossal museum.

"You mean he somehow got out of the building?"

"No, Mariel. Our dear Sunny is...well he's... dead. Since your exhibit is here on the balcony, we decided the noise of the foyer down below should be muffled, given the serious nature of the exhibit. There were some new glass panes put up to keep the noise down as well as shield the tapestries below from fading. It seems our Sunny flew into one and hit it too hard."

"Oh, no...not dead! Oh, that's impossible! *Dead*, Rudy? Not dead...." It was as if the walls of this magnificent and palatial structure had just crumbled on top of her. Mariel felt such a heavy weight and pain in her heart and chest, it actually startled her. Gasping as everything around her seemed to spin, her legs gave way and she sank down to the floor staring in shock. The connection to Sebastian was too close. What did this mean—Sunny—*dead*? She looked to her ring, but nothing. She hoped for a sign, or a word from Rudy that might shed some light in her soul. There was nowhere to turn. The marble floor was cold—like a mausoleum. She did not even have a word or the presence of mind to comfort poor Rudy.

"Oh, Mariel... I am so sorry to tell you this. We all loved Sunny and have never known a bird quite like him in his bold and free spirit. I know how much he meant to you also, after you painted one just like him in your self-portrait. My heart is just sick. We closed off the loggia so that the press wouldn't mob us just yet. The story of

Sunny captured everyone's imagination and got out pretty fast and far. Right now I just don't have the heart to face anyone with this news. Also, I wanted to be the one to tell you first. Mariel, let me help you up. We'll go to my office suite, where you can rest on the couch. Come on, we'll have a little Madeira to calm you down. Poor, sweet, little Sunny.... "

Mariel didn't really hear a word Rudy had said. The universe was spinning cruelly and randomly. How could Sunny be *dead*? How could she feel Sebastian's presence and intervention through this precious creature one day, and a few days later learn that he was dead? Her mind and heart sank into a murky wormhole. Maybe it *was* all her imagination after all. Every dark and despairing thought imaginable overtook her once again, but she was too fragile to recognize the pattern. It was as if the world had suddenly been shrouded by one capricious swath of a black cape, sucking the color and life out of everything! She had probably imagined the whole incident of Sunny out of a need to feel Sebastian near. The fact that this bird happened to fly to her shoulder was a cold, clinical coincidence, random and detached. She felt alone and compressed into a space no greater than a comma in some dispassionate and tragic drama.

"Mariel, drink this. You look pale. It will give you a little perk. I can imagine how you feel, dear. I miss Sunny terribly. I can't tell you what it was like finding that feisty and fearless little bird cold and lifeless on the balcony this morning. It just drained the life out of my veins, Mariel. Why did he have to venture out again, that rascal? And why did they have to put those blasted glass panels up? I just feel sick."

Still in shock, Mariel sipped the sweet Madeira. Why indeed? Why had Sebastian gone to Grozny? Why had he been killed in an explosion? Why was his work seized by criminals? Why were innocent children the pawns of evil and perverse men? Why were they abused and neglected? Why was life so harsh and cruelly senseless? Why had Sunny flown out so hopefully full of life, only to be knocked down dead? Why...? Her thoughts trailed off into hollow oblivion until she realized that Steve had arrived.

"I raced out as soon as I heard, Mari...of all the crazy things... I'm so sorry. Darn it, the news outlets will want your reaction to all of this. Mari, we've got to go over your response. I know this hit you hard."

"Steve...I can't do the interviews. Really, I can't face a camera or the public. I can't do it! Please tell me I won't have to...please. I just want it all to go away. Please, Steve...."

Mariel was now shuddering with tears. It was all just too much.

"Do not worry about a thing, Mari. Rudy, call a cab for us, won't you, and have it pick us up at the private exit. I'll take you back to the hotel, Mari. You should probably take a sedative and rest. We'll talk about everything later. Don't worry about a thing. No one will make you do anything you don't want to. I promise."

"I just can't believe it. Not Sunny, too.... Maybe it's me, Steve. I bring death around me... but why? I just can't stand it any more."

"Nonsense, Mariel. Steve held her limp and faltering shoulders in his strong arms as he locked his gaze on her.

"Mari, Mari, you're *saving* lives! Don't you see that your work has drawn attention *to the problem*? You've broken through what had become an impasse of indifference. Not only are people thinking about human trafficking but also child abuse and endangerment. The latest buzz is that your collection is drawing grieving parents whose children were kidnapped or worse. That is why they put up the glass to muffle the downstairs noise. It seemed insensitive when shattered and broken parents were reliving their tragic losses and searching for a sense of meaning and vindication to hear the drone of jovial banter below. Your work is *life-giving*, Mari, and don't you *ever* doubt it. You are in every way a true artist. The intensity of the past week has left you vulnerable and a bit fragile. I'm so sorry this had to dampen your spirits at a time when you should be celebrating personal triumph and recognition. But, don't let it get to you, Mari. Come on, we'll go back to the hotel for the rest of today."

Chapter Twenty-Three

Plunge

It definitely *had* gotten to Mariel. That much was clear. She knew that Steve was talking, but she hardly heard him. Instead, she felt as if the ground on which she had been standing so confidently had given way and she was plunged into a dungeon of gloom. She had no bearings in the murky darkness where no sound carried, and it was as if the pressure of the earth above was burying her with its density and power.

She didn't remember returning to the hotel, nor sipping some water with a sedative, nor Steve's concerned and abiding presence in the living room of her hotel suite. She was absolutely lost in impenetrable darkness—alone.

Whether real or imagined, she surveyed her situation. She could not tell whether she was standing or lying down. There was no feeling in her feet or anywhere in her body! Was she paralyzed? A chill of terror rippled through her as she began to flail desperately in order to get a sense of her surroundings.

"Ah, at least not paralyzed..." she thought as she threw her arms around and spun wildly. Strangely, she felt nothing, absolutely, *nothing*. She knew she was thrashing around, but did not feel her body, nor the air around it, and much less did she make contact with any surfaces above, below, or around her. All was oppressively black, and unbearably silent. Her movements created no sound— nor did her breathing. Perhaps she had died.

She was aware, but could feel nothing, see nothing, hear nothing—not even herself. While she could picture touching her forehead to see if it was cold or hot, she could not feel her arms move nor her hand touching anything. The darkness was maddening, and completely disorienting. Her screams were inaudible. She imagined that she was plunging deeper and deeper, to more remote and abysmal depths—helplessly isolated and forgotten—cut off and alone. Unfeeling in impenetrable darkness, perhaps she was not really moving at all. She had no way to tell.

As she grew more immersed in the inky pitch of this nightmarish desolation, she thought or imagined a flicker of light. It flitted about (and seemed to be) like a yellow laser point appearing and disappearing in different places. Was it growing larger and getting nearer? It seemed almost like a yellow lightning bug on a summer night. All of her heart and soul rallied for that flicker—yearned for it, and silently screamed out for it. Yes! It *was* growing! It was definitely larger! What could it be?

Did she hear something? Yes! She was certain of it! She heard a strange, smooth sound—perhaps like speech, but not recognizable. It too was distant, but growing.

"Do-ro-ga-va, lyub-i-ma-ya." "Do-ro-ga-va, lyub-i-ma-ya," was the mysterious message. What could it mean?

Frightened and hopeful at the same time, Mariel was

suddenly startled by her recognition of the yellow light! It was *Sunny*! Sunny, but illuminated from within, and pulsing visibly then invisibly in alternating fashion. Simultaneously, the strange message sounded familiar! It was Sebastian's voice—she was certain. There could be no denying it! But what on earth could he be saying?

"Sebastian!" she uttered, or imagined that she did. "Is that you?"

"Mari, Mari, of course it's me. I told you I'd always be near. You are never, ever, *ever*, alone, Mar. No matter what happens, I am near."

"But what is going on?" she bellowed though her voice could not be heard. "Am I dead?"

"Oh, Mar, you're more alive than ever. Let's just say this is like a creative cocoon out of which you will emerge with greater depth and insight. There are many gem babies you have yet to paint, but you needed to feel their helplessness and panic in order to do so. You are safe, and will soon return to your hotel room, which in fact, you never left."

"But why did Sunny have to....?"

"Always, the philosopher...my dear Mari," he observed with the most welcome affection and warmth.

"You must surrender to trust. Nothing is really as bad as it can seem because the Great Lord has the last and final loving word. Surrender, Mari. There are more gem babies. They are waiting to be brought to life by you. Don't ever be afraid. Remember the vapor? Well, that is all it is—vapor. It creates an illusion that a fresh breeze and sunshine are able to dissipate instantly! Be brave, Mari. You are still needed. You have to go back. The Great Lord has plans for you. I will always love you Mari, and I will be there when you need me. One day we will be together again. Sunny is just fine—don't worry. Remember, surrender. You don't need to understand, but to surrender, darling."

That was all she remembered as she began to hear Steve's voice calling to her.

Chapter Twenty-Four

Back Again

"Mariel, are you okay? Mariel, its Steve. You're going to be just fine. Everything is all right. Rudy and I are right here."

As she rubbed her squinting eyes and glanced about, her heart leapt! She could see the bright light coming through the hotel windows! She felt her hands rubbing her eyes, and felt thirsty. She was undeniably alive! Gratefully, humbly alive!

"Steve! It's so good to see you, Steve! And, Rudy, too! I'm here! I'm alive! What happened to me? How did I get back here?"

"Calm, easy...calm, Mariel. Don't try to get up too fast. That sedative did a number on you. Rudy told me that he had given you some Madeira, too—but only *after* I gave you the sedative." Steve shot a chastening glance at Rudy. "We were beginning to worry as you mumbled and groaned in your sleep there. You were so restless, Mariel, we just didn't know what to think. But everything is going to be just fine, now."

"I *have* to paint. There is so much more to do! I don't

know where to start, but I have to start soon! There's more! When can I go back to Boston, Steve? I'd like to get going on this new collection."

"Whoa, just a minute, Mariel. You were *supposed* to have interviews tomorrow. Now, I want you to rest up a bit, until we go to Washington. You haven't forgotten the flash drive, have you?"

"Oh, that's right. Steve, I'm not quite myself yet. It's just that I feel a new painting emerging—like a welcome wave of life. Of course, Washington, Langley and intelligence people.... *Maybe,* and *just possibly*...yes, I remember Steve."

"Here's how it's going down, Mariel. I've cancelled today's interview with *Good Morning America*, and tomorrow's interview with *Fox*. They want to reschedule, but I'm pushing them out until we've been to Washington. That way, there will be some new ground to cover. They'll feel empowered and you'll have a breather. The exhibition still has four weeks at the Metropolitan, so there's no reason we can't space things out a little. The fact that we are perpetuating Sebastian's work will reawaken interest in it, even if we don't mention the flash drive and any new information it might contain. Most of all Mari, don't ever mention that we are getting anything out of Grozny for now. Remember, that is vital."

"Wait a minute, Steve. After Washington, I want to get back to Boston as soon as possible. I'd rather not do any interviews at all. I've *got* to start painting. Why don't you take the interviews? Why do they need me?"

"Well, for one thing you're the artist, and Sebastian's

surviving spouse. For another, you are far more beautiful to look at, as are your paintings."

"Seriously Steve, you could just take it all from the angle of *your* impressions, etc. *You* talk up Sebastian, and when we are ready to launch again, maybe *and the operative word is 'maybe',*" she said with a glint of mischief in her eyes, "then I can come back into the picture. I've had it with the spotlight and the media. Spare me, please. Could I have some ice water?"

"Listen, you need some dinner. Are you hungry? I'm famished and if you prefer we can order-in for tonight. What do you think? I'm ready for some prime rib or something. What do you say, Rudy? Here, I'm pulling up tonight's menu right here. Oooola la! Rack of lamb with gruyère potato gratin, roasted garlic and chestnuts...I'm sold! What about you, Mari? What sounds good? Let's see here... you're a salmon and scallops girl as I recall. How about some seared scallops with risotto and leeks, sweet corn and roasted mushrooms?"

"Sure Steve. As long as we don't have to go anywhere tonight, I wouldn't care if it was cereal and bananas! The scallops sound just fine. Make that—two scallops. Rudy likes the sound of it too."

Perplexed

That evening restored Mariel and encouraged her to enjoy the little time available to drink in the treasures of art New York City held for the next few days. It was Sunday and Mariel found herself at the Metropolitan after closing time, in order to view the Treasures of Terra Gem Exhibition.

Rudy had kindly arranged for her to be here as he often spent the night in the museum anyway—when new exhibits were coming and going. A collection of Victorian gowns and clothing was moving on, and the timing was perfect for Mariel to take her time with the gems, without having to greet those who might have come for her exhibit. Just entering the museum brought with it a panoply of confusing emotions. Her exhibit was on the loggia. There had been that grand and glorious gala, and the abrupt shattering of it by the harsh loss of dear Sunny who had brought to it a unique and consummate triumph. She mustn't forget Sebastian. He was near, and he would help her with the new panels which she felt strangely drawn to painting, but somehow clueless as to how to begin. She felt both weak and tentative, while at the same time, compelled.

Unlike her other depictions, this time she had not seen new gem babies in new mysterious locations. Sebastian had only told her of them. Could she somehow capture the feelings of helplessness and desperation she had experienced in the darkness and bring these gem babies to light? Mariel entered the exhibit hoping to find out.

As she walked past the diamonds, she wondered why she had never seen any gem babies there. The Beryl group caught her interest, in particular the grassy rich, velvety greens. Here was a distinctive color she hadn't really seen with gem babies. Gazing into the verdant tones subtly busy with filigree-like inclusions and what seemed to be an inner glow, she imagined spongy soft, moss paths of an enchanted land, glittering with bright stones like the proverbial Emerald City. Reproaching herself for so romantic a view when she was trying to unlock the faces of helplessly forlorn and forgotten children, she wondered if she just had the wrong color for this collection. After all, in her latest experience the predominating color had been black.

Glancing at the placard near the emeralds she read: "... formed by rising magma and the ensuing metamorphosis...." She felt inspired by the powerful and violent images of molten flows which at once destroyed and recreated all in their path. That might be more like it. But she wasn't ready to paint yet. Somehow, this panel insisted on staying in its undisclosed and nascent state.

As she pensively meandered through the exhibit, Mariel couldn't help thinking of how privileged she was to see each gem as a monument to a forgotten or invisible life. These were not merely adornments or treasures, but signatures and statuary. She wondered what untold stories lay hidden in each exquisite gem. While people had selfishly or sinfully neglected or even harmed the defenseless and innocent, the earth had shown forth immortal trophies in their honor. There was at least a sense of justice in that. It was a world she felt so at home and yet lonely in. The price of a privilege, she mused.

Chapter Twenty-Five

Prelude

Wednesday came soon enough. The flight had been wonderful. Steve worked on his laptop most of the time so that she was free to let her heart and imagination wrestle with the question of how to depict more gem babies. There was something so serene about the uncluttered skyscape. Neither cars, nor buildings, nor roads interrupted the expanse which held them. The sky graciously allowed passage, and soon covered over the path that had been traveled as if to assert its peaceful wholeness. It was a place where thoughts could roam, even if undetected.

In sharp contrast to the peaceful heavens, Washington D.C. on that Wednesday was anything but. The airport was on alert after a suspicious bag had been reported—but not apprehended—in one of the terminal's restrooms. There was a stressful frustration in the air, as airport security, law enforcement, fire rescue and whatever unknown operatives waited tensely for orders. Had it been a hoax, a diversion, or had the wrong person intercepted it? The plane had to land in the cargo terminal with mail carriers. Luggage was unloaded immediately while passengers were asked to remain on the plane. They would be dismissed to waiting taxis as soon as the luggage had been rechecked by airport and homeland security. Thankfully it was a relatively small aircraft which might minimize the delay.

All was done so hastily that they were deplaning in less than forty-five minutes. Once united with their baggage, they were whisked into one of the abundant taxis waiting hungrily for their fares. The tension was only beginning. As they made their way to the hotel, traffic was being rerouted.

"What is going on here?, " Mariel ventured to the dark and swarthy turbaned man who drove their cab.

"Same old, same old," came the surprising retort.

"...Demonstrations heading to the mall. Pro-choice, pro-life—at it again."

As Mariel glanced over at some of the marchers, she was moved to see their faces, and especially the signs they held. Several read: "I regret my abortion." Others, carried by men: "Abortion hurts fathers, too." Another, in banner style showed empty book covers flapping with the caption: "All the biographies we'll never read." She couldn't remember ever seeing any of those in news coverage of such demonstrations.

Mariel ached. If only she could announce to the world: "They are NOT forgotten! Gem babies have stories to tell! Every gem is a monument! Every jewel has a story!" Wishing she had a megaphone the size of her cab, she would tell them all!

"That's it," she thought ecstatically. "That *has* to be it! The timing is no coincidence. Had our flight not been delayed, I might not have seen this group, nor read their signs! That's it! Could it be that the gem babies I did *not* see—but experienced—and have yet to bring to life on canvas, are the very same unfortunate victims of...abortion? The weight of it all nearly took her breath away.

"Un-bee-lee-va-ble!, " slipped from her this time.

"What's unbelievable, Mari? This battle has been on from time immemorial. It's not unlike the moral eclipse which permits human trafficking and child abuse to go on, right under our noses. In fact, that is why our recent success has unsettled certain individuals. I didn't want to mention the bad press we got when you had to deal with the whole Sunny thing, and besides, it's still publicity, which is fine. Well, anyway, we're here. Let's check in, freshen up and choose a place for dinner. Tomorrow is a big day, and I think you should get a good night's rest."

"Rudy mentioned that we had stirred up some controversy by exposing crime, even if my paintings do so in a roundabout way. I suppose we have to expect some of that, don't we? Steve, what would I do without you? You're always looking out for me, aren't you? You've become like my guardian angel. I probably don't thank you enough."

"Guardian is good enough, angel—no. I don't even

know if I like guardian, really. It reminds me too much of the age difference."

"Brother, then? Wise, older brother..."

"Not sure I like that either. Steve is just fine, okay? Come on, let's check out our rooms."

Chapter Twenty-Six

Langley

Morning couldn't come soon enough. In spite of Steve's suggestion, Mariel had not been able to sleep. She wondered what they might learn about Sebastian's work. Would the flash drive give names and places, perhaps? Would this be the long awaited breakthrough? Would Sebastian identify his enemies or murderers, perhaps? She had tossed and turned most of the night, and though tired, was glad to see the morning light streaking through a sliver of space between the heavy hotel curtains. Coffee and breakfast would be arriving with Steve's knock on the door, any time now. She hopped into the shower in order to get ready.

C.I.A. headquarters in Langley, Virginia, was impressive. The cool, crisp, steel and glass structure was strangely ironic. Here, under the disguise of transparency was the most secure and covert operation imaginable. She would have preferred something simpler, but once intelligence was involved, they called the shots. The Senator was excited to see his old friend, and be privy to so fascinating a venture, himself. All were briefed and signed confidentiality agreements. Along with the translation software was an agent who was fluent in Russian, and familiar with the Chechen dialects as well.

Mariel was very familiar with all that Sebastian had discovered so far. This however, was bleakly anticlimactic. The information here was essentially the journal of an undercover agent who was merely tracking the movements of a certain Sergei, along with Korona. It may have provided Sebastian with some patterns and clues but contained nothing particularly damning or explosive. A cross check of locations revealed that these patterns did not point explicitly to holding houses or residences of captives. They were coffee shops and pubs and had been severely damaged in the explosion.

Suddenly, as Mariel was mulling over her disappointment the strange "Dorogava, lyubimaya," came to mind. Why hadn't she thought of this before? What if the words were Russian? Perhaps there was even a clue here!

"Excuse me, Mr. Kansky. I recently heard an expression which may be Russian. Does *Do- ro- ga- va lub- i- ma-ya* sound familiar?"

" Dorogava, lyubimaya, " fell off his tongue like the strong rush of a gurgling stream, and was accompanied by a broad smile. "Your Russian is not bad, actually."

"Good enough to make you smile I see—or is this some good news, or a clue?"

"It means…," (he looked at the men in the room as he hesitated with amusement,) *darling, sweetheart.* Did you hear this in some connection with this information, or…?"

A rush of color came over Mariel as she felt the awkwardness of the moment, and then the pain of separation from her dear Sebastian.

"Oh, never mind...I thought it might be related to our search but apparently it is not."

The flight back to New York was uninterrupted even if restless for Mariel. Steve had tried to compensate for the disappointment with a trip to Tosca, an upscale restaurant recommended in the airline travel magazine as one of the top new places to try but the association with a tragic opera was enough to make Mariel decline. She insisted that Steve excuse her this time. She was consumed by the desire to paint as she longed for the connection to Sebastian, and the imperative to follow his lead in this was a reliable path to that hoped-for connection. Everything else was an unwelcome encumbrance as was the flight which meant more time in New York and *away* from painting. With the evening free, she could at least plan her painting and make some sketches. Steve accommodated—albeit disappointedly. Once he had Mariel safely in the hotel, he called a cab, insisting that he'd bring her take-out as he rambled out the door.

As dear as Steve was, Mariel felt relief with some solitude. At least she didn't have to pretend to be pulled together when she felt near to unraveling. The apparent respite was short lived, however. It didn't take long for that solitude to turn dark again, and come crushing in around her like an imploding building. Would she *ever* know what Sebastian had learned? Would his tragic death be somewhat vindicated by the capture of these ruthless criminals, or would evil triumph, taking more innocent and defenseless children in its loathsome grasp? Clutching her scarf, Mariel bolted out the door, gasping, and without a clue as to where she would go.

Chapter Twenty-Seven

A child interrupts

Mariel had no idea which way and how far she had walked. She had become so enveloped by the tyrannical assault of dark and despairing thoughts that she was oblivious to time or place until she saw a lovely little girl in a red coat, holding her mother's hand while pointing with the other to a large gothic-looking structure. Mariel halted, and breathed deeply. It was a church. The child was pointing to the door. Trusting the "language" of her previous experience in a church, Mariel decided to try the doors, which easily yielded when she pulled at the oversized hardware.

A most warm and inviting glow enveloped the entire place. An organ gently played sacred music. The scattering of people were deep in prayer with heads bowed or staring toward the altar. On the altar was an ornate gold, curiously freestanding object. Though surrounded by lit candles, it was not a candleholder of any kind. The circular center was pure white, but unintelligible to Mariel. The peace, however, was most perceptible. All of the turmoil she had been tossed and whirled in fell off of her like sand under a faucet. She felt the weight of it all lifted, and her heart tranquil. Most of all, she didn't feel alone. She was very much at home, and just sat in a pew for a while, wondering at how differently she felt from mere minutes ago.

As she serenely breathed in the healing glow of this place, a lovely church to be sure, she noticed people standing in quiet thought and single file, outside of two carved doors which opened intermittently to release someone, and receive another person waiting who would close the door behind themselves.

"I wonder if they are going to confession," Mariel considered as childhood remembrances of Grandpa sharing his impressions of the magic and richness of that mysterious encounter scuttled across her mind. Hadn't he told her that when it was time, when she was older, she would understand how wonderful it was? While Grandpa had done his best to share stories of faith with Mariel, her mother at the time was struggling to hold on to faith, and didn't regard herself as the best communicator to a child under those circumstances. Her father had been away so much of her early life, due to his work as a field doctor during the various conflicts in Afghanistan, the Gulf, Iran and Iraq, that she hardly knew him. It was dear Grandpa who had told her how loving God was, how important it was to be good to each other, and to ask for forgiveness when we had gone astray, or guidance when we were lost— from that same loving God. Those simple statements were the only religious tenets of her life, the moral compass that had served her well.

Mariel had never gone to confession. It was rather frightening in a way. At the same time she was drawn to it like a moth to the light. She was in great need of guidance. She hardly knew what to say or how to say it, but she had been tormented with hopelessness so many times that she wondered if one day she might succumb. Would the priest understand? While mulling over these thoughts, a white robed monk, with long beads at his side, opened a door right near her pew. Instinctively, she entered.

Having explained to the priest that she had never been to confession, and that she wasn't really sure what religion she was, but finding herself so often overcome by grief and despair, she just needed some help. Then, with heaving sobs, she poured out her story. The love she and Sebastian shared, his wonderful work, his cruel death, her tumultuous efforts to carry on and the gem baby paintings that had somehow given purpose to her life, as well as some measure of vindication to the cause that she and Sebastian had jointly labored for.

"Are you the artist of those wonderful gem baby paintings, then?" How soothing she found the buttery and kind voice on the other side of the screen.

"Yes."

"Well, then I know exactly what you must do. At all costs, you must continue painting. But, there is more that you need in order to do that, and we should really talk some more. Would you like to come back tomorrow so that we can talk at greater leisure? It is difficult during confession to take the time you deserve in this case. Would 10 A.M. or perhaps 1 P.M. work for you, young lady?"

The kindness in his voice reminded her so much of all that was good and pure—almost like Grandpa, though younger. She desired greatly to meet with him and though her heart leapt at this opportunity, she was too weak to demonstrate her enthusiasm.

"Sure, er...father? " she said haltingly.

"Very well, then. Yes, I am Father Leopold. Come to the parish office next door tomorrow. Now which time would you prefer—ten or one?"

Knowing how prone she was to sleeplessness, Mariel decided it would be safer to choose the afternoon appointment. She received some parting words of blessing, and left the confessional exhausted but light as air, and at peace.

Once outside, she discovered she was at St.Vincent Ferrer church. The taxi soon brought her back to the hotel, where she met Steve who had nearly paced a canyon into the carpet.

"My God, Mariel! Where *were* you? I was worried sick!"

He drew her into his arms with great relief and warmth. "Why didn't you leave a note? I hardly knew where to look, or whether to go or stay. Oh, dear girl, please don't ever do that again!"

"Sorry Steve, it's hard to explain. I went out for a walk and wound up in a church. Actually, it really helped. I'm feeling so much more at peace."

"Well, come over here and enjoy your salmon. Its almond crusted, with sweet potato fries and asparagus. Let me warm it up a bit in the microwave. I ordered some Pinot Grigio for you too. You look as though you could do with a little nourishment."

"Steve...the most wonderful thing happened tonight. Somehow, I know that things will be all right. I actually met a really kind priest, who I plan to see tomorrow. It was as though I was *led* there."

"Let me guess, there was a child somehow involved, right?"

"Exactly! I left here in a horrible claustrophobic anxiety. It felt as though the world had suddenly become nothing but walls closing in on me. I had to leave the hotel for air, and just walked without a clue or plan. I had no idea of anything but my tormenting thoughts until I stopped in my tracks at the sight of a lovely little girl in a red coat. She was pointing to the church. Something inside me just told me to go in."

"Well, all I can say is, someone besides me is surely looking out for you. You end up in the most...well, unlikely places that seem to help nevertheless."

"Steve, this time I felt I was...home. It was different. Fr. Leopold told me I must continue painting, but we're meeting again tomorrow to talk about...things. I'm actually looking forward to it."

"So the interview with PBS...?"

"Steve, I'm *begging* you. Please take it for me. I'm not up to the spotlight—especially not now. I really want to keep this appointment with the priest. Believe me, I might freak out or break down if I went to a studio or anything. I'm just too... fragile right now."

"Okay, okay, my dear. I'll talk to Bruce. Maybe we can reschedule, or if he's okay with me doing the interview, I will. I guess it would be good P.R. for the exhibition. Yep, I guess I had better just do it."

Looking deeply into his grayish green eyes, which betrayed a generous and kindly heart beneath the gruff exterior, Mariel, was so grateful. She leaned over on his chest, and embraced him as a child would, their dad or grandfather.

"Mariel...I've been wondering..."

"Yes, Steve?" Mariel sat up now to look at his expression.

"Do you think there's any chance that you could ever think of me as someone other than a big brother or guardian...?"

The pause hung heavy in the air. Mariel felt totally unprepared for this question, though it had been stirring for some time in Steve's mind.

"Oh Steve, forgive me...you are the kindest, most wonderful and generous man I know today. I've always said, however, that I would never love anyone the way that I love Sebastian, and still do to this day. Please understand, Steve...how grateful I am for all that you have done for me. I care deeply about you, but, well, it's different...." Her voice trailed off with the difficulty of answering his question so suddenly.

"Could it be that you just need more time, Mariel? Do you think there's even a slight chance that in time...?"

"Oh Steve, it would be unfair for me to string you along. All I know is where things stand now, and well, it's just so soon after Sebastian's death—what—a little over a year? I refuse even to consider other possibilities. I couldn't— even with someone as good as you, Steve. I'd be comparing you with him, and I just couldn't keep that up. Please understand that I'd never want to hurt you in any way."

"Yeah, I know, Mari, and it's ok. I'll be here no matter

139

what. What I offer, I offer freely, without expecting in return. While I am older than you, I just couldn't help but ask, since well, I've become very fond of you."

Standing abruptly with a deep breath, he turned to the microwave.

"Some guardian I am! I nearly forgot your dinner. I hope you enjoy it, my dear. Let me pour us both some wine."

Chapter Twenty-Eight

Father Leopold

Mariel found it strangely simple to be on time. She felt light and happy in anticipation of this meeting. Her fears and anxieties had lifted, and even the thought of revealing her innermost thoughts to a perfect stranger, did not create the slightest apprehension. His gentle manner, matched the kindly smile he welcomed her with and confirmed her serenity at this encounter. He was tall and very thin, had grey hair, a mustache and a short beard.

Taking both of her hands in a warm welcome, he turned to walk her down a hall lined with prints of ancient saints, both men and women in white robes with black sleeveless tunics flowing in front and in back. His office was austere. A picture of the Madonna and two saints kneeling beside her, as well as a large and very ancient looking picture of Christ with eyes that seemed to pierce one's soul, were the only adornments to an office with a simple wooden desk and two chairs along with a well packed, and somewhat disorderly case of books. A broad, well used candle burned silently under the Christ picture.

An open Bible lay conspicuously between the two chairs on a simple, round, wooden table.

"It's good to see you this fine morning, young lady. May I offer you some tea or coffee? " was Fr. Leopold's warm salutation.

"Thanks anyway, but I'm just fine...father." Mariel still found it awkward to refer to anyone this way. It was after all, her very first acquaintance with a priest.

"Please make yourself comfortable. I hope that you are feeling better today?"

"It's quite amazing father, but I found such peace in my visit here yesterday, and it hasn't left me."

"Good! I'm very glad to hear that. Now it is a great honor for me to meet such a formidable artist as you, Miss Turner. I was one of the invitees to the original unveiling, since I have been a commentator on religious art for Dominican Studies for some time now. I was most impressed by your work, and by your obvious dedication to so worthy a cause."

"Thank you, Father Leopold. If you're comfortable with it, please call me Mariel. Truly, the honor is mine, but thank you for your kind words. I've had this cause at heart since I was about eleven years old, and dear Sebastian and I felt very strongly about it. Our marriage, in a real sense, was dedicated to eradicating human trafficking in so far as we could. As you know, his efforts in this regard—cost him his life."

"The ultimate sacrifice—for both of you, really."

"Yes, exactly, father. For me now, it is a way to keep Sebastian close. I am anxious in fact, to begin a new series which will represent the victims of abortion."

"I see…that would be a truly noble venture on your part, and a courageous one. I am not certain that all the celebrities and press persons who flocked to you at the gala would remain in your quarter under this banner, however. That is regrettable, and probably more of a knee-jerk reaction than anything, because abortion, like trafficking, child abuse, even endangerment, calls for compassion toward both the child *and* the unfortunate mother. It is, after all, the natural extension of what you have been doing all along.

The church is often misrepresented as somehow insensitive to women by its stance on abortion. However, as Mother Teresa once said: there are two victims in each abortion—the baby *and* the mother. We have to be very compassionate toward the women who opt for this at a time of great vulnerability and even desertion by those who should be there to support them. While the church cannot sanction this choice, it stands with women to bring them to healing and wholeness should they choose it. Most of all, our efforts are focused on avoiding this horrific injustice in the first place through education and a perspective of human sexuality endowed with sacredness from our loving Creator. So, I think you are onto something enormous here, Mariel. After all, how could one deal with violence to innocent children without referring to the most pervasive and statistically costly of *all* violence?"

"I see that this might be more complex than any of the other gem baby paintings. I hadn't thought of their mothers and how they could feel singled out and harshly judged by putting the spotlight on this unfortunate reality."

"Yes Mariel, compassion is our first rule. We work for

truth and speak the truth, but always in charity. That is, lovingly—never as judges. These women bear the wounds of their unfortunate decisions all their lives, and even those who adamantly defend this choice, must be met with compassion, even pity—and *not* with blame."

"Father Leopold, I have never heard such loving sentiments expressed as beautifully as that!"

"Well, don't credit me for that last sound byte. A woman from the 12th century, known as Julian of Norwich deserves the credit for that one. I'm just fond of her writings, and perhaps you would be too. Yes, the church must have its arms of unconditional love always ready to embrace all those who are bowed down even by their own sins, because, truth be told—that's all of us, Mariel. So, even your paintings must treat the walking-wounded mothers delicately and without judging them. This is what it means to build a *culture of life*."

"What a beautiful expression—*the culture of life*! I must say father, it is a known fact that the Catholic Church has stood all kinds of opposition in its defense of human life in modern times. With your explanation I am realizing that the Catholic Church stands with women too, even as it defends the defenseless children. I guess it was just a matter of time before I put two and two together and had this conversation, which mysteriously, I seemed led to through some kindly and I would venture to say, heavenly intervention."

"Miss Turner, excuse me...Mariel, you are right about the Church standing boldly in season and out of season— even if alone and ridiculed, maligned and berated, in defense of the sacredness of all human life, but this is a very old battle—not just one waging in modern times. In fact, writings exist from the first century, testifying to the fact that in the pagan Roman Empire, Christians were easily identifiable as the only ones who would risk their lives to rescue the unwanted and abandoned children left to die of exposure in the deserted outskirts of the main population centers. It was for acts such as this that they earned the distinction of "see how they love one another." Do not forget that their example coexisted in a time of oppression, slavery, exploitation, war, and even violent arena games in which Christians were hunted down to their deaths as an entertainment spectacle."

"I didn't realize that, father. That is truly incredible—horrific, really."

"Yes, the church has stood for life—consistently for the two thousand plus years since our Lord Jesus walked among us. And we shall continue to do so. That is why I wish to support you in any way I can to continue your work."

"I am so grateful for your support father. I especially want to carefully consider how best to draw in the "walking wounded" as you called them…the mothers who lose so much by one terrible mistake. I will give that expression "pity and not blame" some thought and try to portray it somehow. For some reason, I just don't know how to begin."

"Well, Mariel, you definitely have a gift, and I am sure that you will find a way. For now, I will pray that you find that way. I will always be here for you—anytime, so, do *not* hesitate to call. Oh, and Julian said that *the Lord* looks on us with pity and not with blame. It is what we need to imitate as well as remember, since we all share the human condition."

"Thanks so much Father. Maybe that will get me going—the prayers, that is. I'll keep you posted, and thanks for your time."

"God bless you, Mariel. He is blessing you right now, and is always near. Come back next week and I should have an extra copy of Julian of Norwich for you. Perhaps it will help with the painting."

"That would be great father! I never thought it would be so easy to talk to a priest, and I feel so fortunate to have met you."

"Oh, I try, but you are too kind. Mariel, it's all about baby steps really...in imitation of the Great Lord."

Chapter Twenty-Nine

Great Lord

Mariel could not stop thinking of the emphasis Fr. Leopold put on those two words—Great Lord—the very words used by the gem babies. His broad and pensive smile, arched eyebrows and solemn tone were protecting some deeper sense, but it seemed premature to ask the question now. How did he come to use that particular term? Mariel didn't think it was a common expression even among believers, and yet he seemed to emphasize it like a secret password. Too surprised and shy to inquire, she left pondering. What a wonderful and mysterious encounter! How amazing that she came to meet him in the first place.

The week was a frustrating mixture of unsatisfying sketches and plans; it was clear that Mariel had met painters' block. More than anything she wanted the feel and smell and immersion into paint and canvas, but she was still in Manhattan, and would be a little longer. She felt uncomfortably detached from Sebastian, but encouraged by her new friendship with Fr. Leopold.

"That's it!" she thought. I need to see Fr. Leopold again.

He told me to come back. Maybe that writer…Julian would help!"

After securing an appointment time, Mariel set out happily. Fr. Leopold invited her to enter the church from the office passageway, where he brought her to a side chapel adorned with a lovely Madonna. He first knelt serenely and silently in profound prayer, then gently rose to take her back to the office. Mariel was enraptured by the peacefulness in the Madonna's face and expression, and the beauty of motherhood it depicted.

As they entered his humble office again, Fr. Leopold lit up with a smile.

"I have the book for you, Mariel. Please keep it with my blessings. I think that Julian's perspective will serve you well. In any case, I hope it will and would look forward to hearing your reactions, when and if you would like to share them."

Mariel glanced at the paperback which seemed to have short vignettes with title headings. Her eyes landed on a particular phrase.

"You seem interested already, Mariel."

"Oh, yes, thank you Fr. Leopold. I was looking forward to the book and randomly stumbled on Julian saying "All shall be well, and all shall be well and all manner of thing shall be well." It really resonated for some reason, as if it was meant for me at this time.

"I would argue, that it was not randomly," quipped father with his usual kindly smile.

"Fr. Leopold…I mentioned to you last time that I felt *led* here. I had no plan to come to this church and would have raced right past it had it not been for a child pointing to it. As you know, I never intended to enter the confessional either, and didn't even realize that there was one right near me until you opened it and that little green light went on. Now I feel a sense of purpose and resolution, and well, blessing if you will—to continue on my path. Actually it's more than that really. It is as though I was meant to come here all along, and well, that is rather unsettling in a way. It's as though a whole new world lies open to me, and I can't believe I've just stumbled on the threshold of it, as if by some greater plan or destiny."

"Life is a mysterious adventure, isn't it Mariel? As one of my favorite rather contemporary writers, Thomas Merton once wrote: *"We are living in a world that is absolutely transparent, and God is shining through it all the time."* I believe that you *have* been led here. Furthermore, it was not random, but rather, a part of the custom designed master plan of a loving God—yes, the Great Lord who cares very much about you."

"Okay, now I *have* to ask you. How is it that you use that term…the *Great Lord?* I don't hear other Christians or Catholics use it really, though everyone knows it means—God. You said it last time, and with what seemed to me some implied emphasis, and again today…father."

After a reflective pause, Fr. Leopold drew a breath.

"Mariel, let me tell you a story. It's my story. It has everything to do with why I don't believe any of this is accidental or random.

When I grew up in the Catskills with my three brothers and older sister, we lived near a lake. All summer long we'd go down to it, sit on the dock and fish, dive in and swim, or take out the row boat. One morning Johnnie and I got up before dawn so that we didn't have to take our baby brother Max with us. We wanted to do some fishing out in the middle of the lake, but it was hard with a little brother who couldn't handle a fishing pole or have the patience and attention to wait for a bite. I guess we were being a little selfish, though we fully intended to get back before he knew we had gone.

Well, the way he looked up to us, it was if he had radar or something, and no sooner had we left than he ran out after us. When we had left the dock and rowed out about a hundred feet or so, we saw him jumping and screaming for us to come back. We told him to wait, and so he did. Disconsolately, he sat in a heap on the dock, pouting as little brothers can do when feeling left out. It didn't dawn on us that he wasn't wearing the life jacket we usually made him put on at the lake. We were too engrossed in some serious bass fishing. The next time we looked up at him, now from much farther out, he was leaning over the edges of the dock, trying to stir the water with his fingers. We called out to him to stop, but were out of range. He must have been fascinated by a fish, or a minnow, or maybe his reflection, because within the next few seconds he leaned over so far that he tumbled off the dock and fell into the water.

Horrified, we rowed back like madmen, but...we were too late. Little Max drowned that day, and well, our lives would never be the same.

I was about twelve and Johnnie was fifteen. It was as if the sun had stopped shining. We couldn't look each other in the eye. We didn't even want to see the lake again. In fact, our family ended up moving. Johnnie took it especially hard since he was older and should have noticed that Max didn't have his life vest on. I was despondent. My grades dropped, and I felt that life had ended. It had in a way. The simple carefree life of a mountain boy had ended. Soon I would find out that a new life was opening up.

When we moved to the city, my parents put me in a Catholic school. That is what saved me, I suppose, though the grief never really left me. One thing led to another, and I entered the seminary. It was as I prepared for ordination and spent an entire night in prayer, that I had an extraordinary experience. I must have fallen asleep. After all, we rose at five, had an intense day and there I was praying through the night or trying to, at least. All I know is that I had the most wonderful and what would be the most liberating dream I could ever imagine.

I *saw* little Max. He came to me in prisms of light and color. There were layers of glorious laughter and glee, and amazing music. He hugged me and told me never to be sad again. He was with the Great Lord and I shouldn't blame myself or Johnnie for what had happened. The Great Lord was so kind and loving, he could never be happier, and in fact, insisted that I patiently prepare to join him some day. I remember it as if it was yesterday. He said: 'I used to run after you and Johnny. But the Great Lord sent me to tell you that you would follow me in time.' That was over twenty years ago."

"So, you have seen the...gem babies, too Father?"

"Yes, I suppose I would have to agree to the extent that I saw Max at least, though it's hard to explain whether it's all a dream at times. Also, I honestly don't remember gems, Mariel, but just infusions of flashing and sparkling light.

What I hold onto is that these holy innocents point to and remind me of the goodness of our God.

Most of us are very unaccustomed to the idea of death. In other cultures it is seen as the corridor to a new life. Actually, that is a very Christian view, but as moderns, we are uneasy with it. We like to think we are in control, and yet death comes with an annoying finality, without consulting us, as it were. Max and your gem babies remind us that it is all a message of hope really. We are destined for another life, where there is no pain or suffering, where good is rewarded and justice served.

In spite of any tragedy, good *does* triumph, and we need to see ourselves on a journey with these innocent ones who are happy and in heavenly peace. They have no anger or judgment toward anyone. Their hearts are free and loving—fully forgiving. The Great Lord makes sure that they are happier than any of us could make them or imagine, in spite of the wrong they have suffered at the hands of those who should have cared for them.

That is why I was so taken by your paintings, Mariel, but I never dreamed that you had entered that realm and were, so to speak, reporting back."

"Amazing, Father! And I never thought that anyone would know from experience that my paintings represented what I believe—even if I don't really comprehend it all—to be that *great* reality."

Mariel straightened up a bit as she took in a deep reviving breath. She thought for a moment about Sebastian and that he would probably like Fr. Leopold a great deal.

"Now you see how I could never think of our meeting as random or accidental, Mariel. Before I had that dream it was Julian of Norwich who somehow spoke to my heart in the most healing and reassuring tones. Oh, as the years poured out I embraced the notion that God would take care of little Max. I found comfort in following Christ and had faith that I was called to living by his word and sacraments. But I never knew that my own wounds could be assuaged, and the pall of guilt and sadness lifted. It is not accidental that your eyes fell on the very lines that stirred a much deeper faith in me: 'All shall be well.' Those of us tried in the fire of loss and tragedy need those words. It is also comforting to know that others know the pain we have experienced. That fact offers the hope of solidarity and profound understanding. In a way, that can seem to compensate us for the deficit and loss."

Tears like a rising tide had begun to flow from Mariel's eyes again. It was overwhelming for her to realize just how miraculous this encounter was. Not only did she find a deeper and richer approbation of her life's labors, but it was as if a giant stone had been rolled away,and a bright light was dawning with unknown but loving promise. There seemed to be a deeper meaning and a profound connectedness to all that had happened in her life. She saw herself as a tiny leaf, fragile, veined and pigmented— inconspicuously common and unremarkable among the millions that fall so quietly on a forest floor or the water's edge. That tiny leaf floated down a gentle stream, transporting her quite deliberately, and somehow she felt the embrace of meaning and compassion enveloping her and enfolding her. She nearly swooned from the weight that seemed to lift from her usually heavy heart. She heard

Sebastian's words again and seemed to understand them for the first time: "Surrender."

"Oh, my poor girl! Allow me to offer you some tissues. Are these tears of sorrow, wonder, or perhaps, joy?"

"All of the above, father. I'm just so...overwhelmed... but in a good way. I don't think that I ever experienced and recognized God's involvement so *personally* in my life until this very moment. In fact, until now I would not have attributed it to God's presence at all. This is all so sublime and incomprehensible. Also, for the first time I feel sufficient trust to just surrender to it, though I have no idea where it will lead."

"Well, have no fear there. The Great Lord—our precious Lord Jesus—will take you to his own loving heart, and there is no need to worry about that!"

Mariel just stared into his good and loving eyes. He really believed that, and while his belief did not convince or transform her, she found strength in it nevertheless. How grateful she was for this wonderful priest! How she marveled at the miracle of intervention that her meeting with him had wrought. How open and trustful of the future she now felt! That in itself was an enormous shift from her usual temperament and perspective. She was literally swept off her feet, but was lovingly held up in a new kind of assurance and peace. Never could she have anticipated anything so wonderful.

"Do you like poetry, Mariel?"

"Actually, I do."

"May I read you a poem?"

"Of course, father. I'd love that."

Let me find it here in my favorite anthology. Here it is.

"*The Kingdom of Heaven*" is its name. Francis Thompson, a rather conflicted but loving soul, offers a unique glimpse of that transparency I mentioned earlier. Let's see if you like it. Oh, one thing—when he talks about Charing Cross, it's a train station and bridge commonly known in London. You probably recognize Thames as the river that traverses London. Thompson is an Englishman, so his references are meant to evoke very familiar landmarks at home. Think of it the same way that we here in New York might say the Hudson River or the George Washington Bridge. There is also Gennesareth, otherwise known as the Sea of Galilee. That is a frequent reference in the Bible as Jesus found himself there on numerous occasions. It was the same body of water he calmed, and the one Peter attempted to walk on at his bidding. I don't want you to trip up at the crescendo of the poem for lack of reference on those points. Ready?"

"Please go ahead. I'm ready."

Father began in his gentle but emphatic voice, uttering each line with such appreciation that Mariel could not but feel that this was going to be another sacred moment in an extraordinary day.

The Kingdom of God

O world invisible, we view thee,
O world intangible, we touch thee,
O world unknowable, we know thee,
Inapprehensible, we clutch thee!

Does the fish soar to find the ocean,
The eagle plunge to find the air—

That we ask of the stars in motion
If they have rumor of thee there?

Not where the wheeling systems darken,
And our benumbed conceiving soars!—
The drift of pinions, would we hearken,
Beats at our own clay-shuttered doors.

The angels keep their ancient places—
Turn but a stone and start a wing!
'Tis ye, 'tis your estrangèd faces,
That miss the many-splendored thing.

But (when so sad thou canst not sadder)
Cry—and upon thy so sore loss
Shall shine the traffic of Jacob's ladder
Pitched betwixt Heaven and Charing Cross.

Yea, in the night, my Soul, my daughter,
Cry—clinging to Heaven by the hems;
And lo, Christ walking on the water,
Not of Gennesareth, but Thames!

Mariel was stunned by the drama and images evoked. She asked to read it to herself again. Her heart seemed on fire, as she sensed it almost beating out against her ribs.

"I love this poem! What a man! He paints with words… and amazingly! He describes the world as we know it, embedded with mystery and wonder beyond what we first see—as far beyond it as the moon and stars from where we sit right now. That is how it truly is, I'm discovering. But father, at the end is he saying that in our darkest times, when our soul cries out in anguish, that Christ comes to us...*wherever* we are?"

"Precisely, Mariel—with pinpoint accuracy at the precise time, and in the particular manner we need the most. Have you *not* experienced that, Mariel?"

"Well, to be honest father, I've experienced extraordinary things in the gem babies and all, but I am not so ready to conclude that it was Jesus who was making it all happen...."

"And just who do you think the Great Lord might be?"

"I don't know, really—some magical king almost."

"And so he is, and infinitely more! He is a loving Savior. He lays down his life for us out of love, and without any expectation of return. You *must* come to know Jesus, and then you will understand better who *you* are and the beautiful mingling of meaning and mystery enfolded into your very being. In a sense you do know him, in your inmost heart of hearts, but it seems you have not developed the relationship. Are you baptized, Mariel?"

Mariel was surprised that she didn't really know.

"Um... I'm not really sure, father. My grandfather was a Catholic and loved to talk to me about God, but he died when I was very young. We never really went to church or anything. I know my mom would pray when she was upset with my father being in combat zones with no ability to contact him. She never really talked to me about it, though. I suppose I'd have to ask her. Aren't people baptized when they are babies?"

"Well, it all depends on whether the parents ask for it, in the case of a baby. But as adults, people are baptized at any time they are ready, and desire it. Perhaps you can ask you mother if you were baptized, and where and when that might have been. Wouldn't that be good to know, Mariel?"

"Sure, father. It would! I just never thought of it before. I'll have to call my mom and find out."

"Do that Mariel, and we'll talk again. By the way, how are you getting along with Julian of Norwich?"

"Oh! Actually, I like her a lot. The picture she paints of…God—Jesus, I guess—is very loving, kindly, and well, so comforting. In many places, he seems to be a gentleman. When she talks about his suffering for us, well, it's hard to understand, and yet it quiets my soul at the same time. It helps me when I agonize over the innocent children who are victimized by violence, abuse, trafficking. Frankly, I never thought that God who *didn't have to suffer* had undergone so much! It leaves the whole question of why innocent people suffer at all—suspended in a kind of space and time warp—where He seems to take it all in…. It's hard to explain, but am I getting it right, father?"

"Oh, I think you're doing very well Mariel. That is why I say that in your heart of hearts you do know Him. He is just, as it were, recessed and shrouded since you have not learned the Scriptures or what the two thousand year meditation of the church has produced to shed light on who He is. But not to worry, your instincts are very good. Furthermore, He is far more approachable and accessible than you might imagine.

For now, I suggest that you continue to read Julian, and today, I'd like to give you this small New Testament. Mariel, you might consider coming to a Bible study or something to help you along. It's one thing to plod through

on your own—and that is a valuable practice—but quite
another to break it open with others who, like yourself, are
new to the exploration. How does that sound?"

"Well, I'm not sure how much longer I'll be in New
York father, but it sounds good."

"Take this schedule with you, and see what works for
you. The Tuesday night group is largely made up of young
professionals like yourself. You might be most comfortable
there, but I'll leave that up to you entirely."

"Thank you, Father. I feel so fortunate to have you as
a sort of guide. I'll see what I find out about my baptism,
and...could we talk again?"

"Certainly, Mariel. I'll be away next week, but after
that I'd be happy to meet with you again. See Jody at the
front desk. She has my calendar. I don't trust my memory
that far into the future for a minute. She'll give you some
choices, and yes, let's talk again. God bless you. If I may,
I'd like to suggest that you go to the chapel for a few
minutes. Just stay and talk to God as you would to a loving
father—the Great Lord who loves with the most tender and
pure love. How does that sound?"

"Sure, father. I just never thought of it without a child
pointing to the church or something, but sure!"

"After all, perhaps the gem babies have been leading
you to church doors for some time..." he said with his
usual kindly smile, as he stood to lead Mariel to the door.
"God is always near, and blessing you."

"Thanks, father. See you when you get back."

Chapter Thirty

Surprise Visit

So many thoughts were swirling in Mariel's mind that she needed quiet and time to sift through them. Wow! Little had she known that this prolonged New York stay would afford her the chance to meet Fr. Leopold, who not only knew and appreciated her art, but had experienced the same loss and accompanying comfort which the story of the gem babies provided. How different things now were from the night she had blustered into the church after being tormented by dark and suffocating thoughts! What a sense of peace, along with a kind of beckoning from the horizon of mystery and meaning, now pulsed through her. She felt alive and hopeful again! Strangely, this had all served to calm her down while she experienced the "hold" on her desire to paint. Her soothed mind and heart leapt to instant alert as she inserted the key card in her hotel room door and bolted to answer the ringing phone.

"Hello," she gasped.

"Mar, its mom!"

"Mom! What a nice surprise. But is everything all right?"

"Oh, yes Mar, don't you worry. I've never been better. In fact, I have some amazing news for you," she taunted mischievously.

"Tell me mom. Really I wouldn't have a clue.... What is it?"

"I'll be in New York...are you ready? *Tomorrow*, Mar!"

"What? Are you serious, mom? How did you swing that?"

"Well, I finished the semester, and you should be proud of me. I'm now a bona fide LPN. To celebrate, I thought I'd like to see my girl and pop the cork right there in New York City! I'll arrive at JFK at 2:40 in the afternoon tomorrow. Should I take the shuttle, or a cab?"

"Mom, you are blowing me away. This is great, and really a surprise! I have so much to tell you and show you, and well, it's far better in person, so this is great! Let me talk to Steve. Knowing him, he'll send a limo, and you'll see your name held up by a suited chauffeur as you come down for your baggage. Let me call him now, since the time is so short. Can I call you right back?"

"Sure, Mar, but a limo...? Maybe we shouldn't bother Steve."

"Nonsense, mom. If I kept this from him and he found out that you took a cab, he'd actually be *offended!* That is just how he is. Trust me on this. The man is just incredibly kind and generous."

"And, sweet on you, Mar. You must know that. Any progress I should know about?"

"Mom, please stop right there. He's just like that. I'll call you right back. And there will be no discussion of anything along *those* lines, promise?"

"I just don't understand you sometimes, Mariel. Okay, okay, but you don't have to clam up this way, or put the kabosh on any mention of what everyone but you seems to think is obvious and actually a very *good* thing...."

"Mom, I'll call you right back. But promise me mom—I won't hear another word about this when you come—okay? I want this to be a happy visit. Really, I'm looking forward to it, so...let's not ruin it...promise?"

"Okay, okay. Geez! Why do I feel like I'm signing a severance? Okay. I'll let it be." Clearly exasperated, but wanting to restore her equilibrium Rosie continued: "You do have a pull-out couch or something, right? I was thinking I'd just stay with you, if that's okay."

"No problem, mom. I can do better than that but even if I had to sleep on the floor I'd want you here with me. You didn't stay long enough after the gala, and we have *so* much to talk about. Don't worry, there is a pull-out, and you can have my bed. It's more than enough, you'll see."

"Great, Mar. Let me know what Steve says. I'm home packing now, so call me back tonight. If he isn't able to arrange something, I want to call for a shuttle before I leave tomorrow morning. So call me back as soon as you can."

"Okay, mom, talk to you later. And don't worry. Steve always comes through."

Mariel was lucky enough to catch Steve as he headed to a board dinner she had declined to accompany him to. It was all arranged. Louie would be at the terminal and would bring Rosie to Mariel's hotel where she and Mariel would share a suite. Quite an upgrade, and with a completely great view! Steve would meet them for dinner and a royal New York City night tour tomorrow. Whew! How fast things seemed to be racing! Mariel would move out of her private room in the morning in preparation for her mom's stay. Yes, Steve was very kind to her. Fighting back the tension of knowing his hopes, she remembered how unconditionally he had pledged himself to her. Together they were champions on behalf of invisible crime victims, and that was enough for her.

Chapter Thirty-One

A shocking turn

Mariel moved to the suite which Steve leased all year long in the event that friends, family, or associates came to visit. Louie dropped off the key right after leaving Steve at the office. As it turned out, Mariel's room on the seventh floor was paid for the rest of the month, so there was no need to completely move out. She could just stay upstairs while her mother was in town. After a mid morning run, a shower and early lunch, Mariel took a few things up to the twelfth floor suite and took out her copy of Julian of Norwich.

"If there is anywhere on earth a lover of God who is always kept safe, I know nothing of it, for it was not shown to me. But this was shown: that in falling and rising again we are always kept in that same precious love."

She was lurched from her tranquil basking by tremulous shaking and a loud noise. Too stunned to move, she waited until a piercing alarm followed by instructions over some sort of P.A. system alerted everyone to evacuate the building *immediately*, by the east elevators. No one was to use the stairs or any other elevators. Mariel gathered up her sketchbooks and a jacket, and left immediately. She met with the same bewildered looks and edgy questions everyone had on the elevator. It seems that a fire had started—possibly from an explosion on the seventh floor. No one knew any more. Mariel couldn't help but think that only this morning she had awakened on the seventh floor. Had it not been for her mother's imminent visit, she would have been there, and…what then?

The hotel lobby was buzzing with firemen, police, and hotel staff ushering the guests to the sister hotel across the street for hospitality while things got sorted out. No one made a statement. All the guests stayed glued to the news station in the coffee shop, and within the hour were shocked to see their very hotel lobby on the television screen. It had been a bomb! No one had claimed responsibility, and the damage was too extensive to find any fingerprints but there was an investigation of the possibility that the flowers delivered to room 712 shortly after twelve noon had disguised a bomb which went off at 12:45 PM, when housekeepers went into the room to freshen it. One was killed on impact, and the other suffered serious burns and had been rushed to the hospital. Apparently the mechanism was motion triggered and detonated. The name of the guest who was not in the room at the time was being withheld until located… Mariel's heart raced and her feet turned to lead as she stopped hearing the news feed. 712 was *her* room, or had been until she moved to the 12th floor in preparation for her mom's visit. Stunned and frozen, she hardly heard her cell phone ringing until the kindly woman seated next to her nudged her and asked,

"Is that your phone, sweetie?"

It was Steve.

"Oh, Mariel, *Thank God* you're okay! I nearly died of a heart attack when Suzanne told me she had heard there was a bomb in your hotel! You're 100% fine, right? Where are you? I'm coming right over!"

After a stunned silent pause, Mariel replied: "It was a bomb, Steve, in my room."

Steve gasped, and his breathing betrayed that he was running.

"Mariel, wait for me right where you are. Don't move, or talk to anyone. I'm on my way! I'll meet you in the coffee shop. They have you across the street, right?"

Steve made it to the Down Urban Hotel in record time. Mariel was in shock and hardly heard anything around her.

After a reassuring embrace, Steve whispered,

"Let's get out of here. I don't want your picture in the media, which will make access all the easier. The police want to question you now, but I arranged for a remote video chat, due to your present state of shock, and the possible dangers of visibility. I'm taking you to my place out on the Island. "

Mariel was too stunned to respond, but was inwardly glad that someone was thinking for her.

"I parked the Porsche out front, since Louie's at the airport. I told him not to tell your mother anything if she didn't already hear of it, which she may not have, given the flight restriction on electronics. The short flights don't even offer the usual media feeds you otherwise find. Let's hope she doesn't know. Anyway, I've instructed him to bring her to my place in the Hamptons. It's only about an hour and a half from Kennedy. We'll meet them there, and can hold the video conference there. No one at the office needs to know where I'll be, as long as they can reach me any time. We need time to talk and think."

Leaving wasn't quite as simple. Police were outside the coffee shop and requiring that each person be checked against a list of hotel guests from across the street. All guests were to remain where they were until detectives and attorneys arrived for questioning each. When Steve presented the scanned waiver he had received electronically from the captain, the officer on duty insisted on calling it in to be sure. He was about to do so when he was ordered to join two senior officers as they huddled near the media pool. Excusing himself, and leaving them in limbo, the officer promised to be back soon. His replacement claimed that it was not his call, and that they'd just have to sit tight. Steve was frustrated and about to express his impatience when the officer's attention was diverted to the foyer, where several people had clustered around a frail woman who had apparently fainted, and might need medical attention. Sensing a window of opportunity, Steve jumped at it.

"Mariel, we're in luck. If you go to the ladies room, there is a door to the sidewalk patio seating area. I don't think they have that covered right now, and if they do, I'll think of something. Leave that way, and I'll have the Porsche there in about five minutes. Can you do that Mar?" His eyes were bright with adrenaline and compassion. He loved coming to her rescue, and just looking into his eyes convinced her of how much she needed his strength right now.

"Yes, Steve. I'll be there. I'll be okay—go ahead."

In his usual quick thinking style, he had padded the doorman's palm with a few of the Benjamins he carried like most people carried ones or fives, so that he would assure the police that the car would be gone before it could be towed. Sure enough, Steve was able to clear the police barricade, just as the doorman was being overruled by a policeman ordering that a boot be placed on one of the Porsche's tire rims, so that it could not be moved until towed. He was in a bad mood and would not make any exceptions.

"I'm so sorry for the trouble, officer. I know someone who works here and just wanted to check on them. Along with my apologies, please accept my donation for the Police Athletic League. It won't happen again."

The bills worked their magic once again. Won over before he could object, the officer ordered the installer of the tire boot away. Caught off guard he chortled,

"Yeah, make sure it doesn't happen again...okay, thanks for your support, but make sure I don't see that car out here again!"

Waving Steve off, he turned to the screeching bullhorn across the street.

Given the fact that her hotel was swarmed with firefighters, a hazmat team, concerned family and friends all clamoring for information—the place was a hive of tension. Reporters and television cameras had been left to curbside speculation as to what was being discovered. Now, they were being told that the Chief of Police would hold a press briefing at 4 P.M. to update them. Aside from the two housekeeping personnel, it seemed there were no other injuries, but the investigation was still underway.

Surveillance cameras were being studied in hopes of identifying the bomber. Given the entrance, lobby and elevator cameras, as well as those in the guestroom hallways, they should have something. All questions would have to wait until 4 pm, it seemed.

Sure enough, Steve was shaking hands with the young officer outside the sidewalk exit of the café. He too had received a surprise donation for the Police Athletic League and had learned that Steve's co-worker just happened to be in the coffee shop when all the guests from the Metro Towers across the street came in. She was cleared to leave.

Stunned out of protocol, and easily persuaded by this generous donor, the young officer stammered:

"Well, if she's cleared, it should be fine. What did you say her name was?"

Breaking the vigorous double handshake which had overpowered the policeman, Steve sputtered:

"There she is, oh Brenda, yes it's Brenda, Brenda Sturgess," and with eyes that demanded she play along, he started rushing her into the car.

"Brenda, so glad you're out of that mess—we're late for the meeting... Thanks, officer. As always, it's a pleasure seeing New York's finest here for our protection. Thankfully, we're all okay."

Like a stuntman he was off in a flash, leaving the rookie wondering whether anyone had seen this exchange.

Chapter Thirty-Two

Safe Refuge

"Whew! For a minute there I thought they had us. Mar, relax if you can. I'm here and you're going to be all right."

Pressing a button released the mini-bar. "Mar—go ahead. Have a bourbon or something. You look like a ghost."

With a deep and tired sigh, she replied, "I think I will. It's hard to believe I was really targeted."

"Mar... I do have some things to tell you, but not till I see that you've had at least half of that drink. Go ahead. Just press the ice button and the tray will slide out... there you go. I wish I could join you, but this time I'm the driver."

Traffic was abysmal, and it would take longer to get to the Hamptons than usual. Relaxed but perplexed by Steve's remark, Mariel braced herself.

"What exactly do you have to tell me Steve? You know something? Steve, I expect full disclosure, so let me have it!"

"Mar, there were threats at the Metropolitan. You've

been so fragile through all of this I didn't feel the need to tell you, especially since the police and Langley were sorting it out. It could be a prankster, or publicity stunt."

"...Threats!" Her head started to pound. "What kind of threats?"

"It could just be some idiot. They threatened to leave a bomb in the Metropolitan unless the exhibit was pulled. Well, with the Van Goghs, Rembrandts, and Monets in the place, it is already secured with a very sophisticated surveillance system."

Steve was speed talking.

"There isn't an inch of the place a camera can't see, so it seemed highly unlikely that anyone would succeed, if they managed to get through the security at the door *and* the motion detectors. Really Mar, airports should have what that museum has in terms of screening devices. I didn't think you needed to know anything until we had some sort of certainty."

He thought of her tenderly. He was her protector and guardian. He would keep her safe. As he found the fastest lane to the Queensboro Bridge, he engaged even more of the adrenaline he needed to maneuver the Porsche and keep up the conversation while navigating from the GPS, with the motive of keeping Mariel calm and secure.

"Did the threats mention me in particular?"

"No. That was puzzling. Also, since you haven't been doing the TV interviews, there was no reason for anyone to know that you're here, in New York. You've been spending your time at that church, and have been really low key. We thought it was someone annoyed with ICC, or I would have had you trailed. Anyway, I'm not taking any chances. The compound in South Hampton is very safe. Oh, that's Louie now. They must have arrived."

"Great, Louie. Does she know anything? Good. If at all possible, keep her from the television. Make her comfortable. Start a fire, pour her a drink, sit on the porch and watch the sunset. We're stuck on the expressway and its log jammed. I should have taken a chopper."

South Hampton

Rosie lost no time in acclimating herself to the posh ocean front compound. The rolling breakers could be heard through the screened panels, which also admitted the sea air washing over all with freshness and life. The sky was a palette of bright orange and blue, reflected on the satiny waters which sparkled with every fiery hue.

"You know, Louie, I had no idea Steve had a place like this. Mariel tells me so little, even though I'm her mom. How long have you known Steve?"

Louie took a deep breath and looked at the ceiling. His trim build and just as trim beard lent a fastidious air to the otherwise open and friendly man before her.

"Let me see…I knew him before his wife died… so that has to be over ten years now."

"Steve is a widower? What happened?"

"Actually, it was tragic. Justine, who was a model, and in the Caribbean on a shoot, took an excursion one afternoon—scuba and sailing. Well, there was an accident and both she and one of the divers were killed. You may remember the celebrity papers. Justine Wilton, daughter of John Wilton, who made his millions on security systems patents and still does, was dead. Everyone was talking about it. Pretty sad, really, but—don't tell Steve I told you—the marriage was on the rocks anyway. They had been living separate lives for over a year, and, well, she wasn't very faithful. Steve always was. Good Jewish boy, you know. Though he got the shaft, he kept up appearances, and just kept very, *very* busy. They didn't have any kids. She was away so much anyway, (which probably contributed to it), but there were drugs—you know the modeling scene—and I guess she was lonely. Anyway, though he grieved, it was different for Steve. He grieved for what *could have been*, but not what actually was, if you know what I mean. He never remarried, though he could have had almost any woman he wanted. Somehow, he just settled into work, and seemed to find solace in helping desperate and trafficked kids. He wanted to make a difference and still does. I'll tell you though, I think he's wild about your daughter. It has given him a spark and fresh take on things. At first it was all just paternal—he is so protective. But I think that if he had his way...things would progress, if you know what I mean. He confides in me a lot, and I think that he is one of the best human beings alive—bar none. Someone with Steve's wealth and integrity is a rare find. He's extraordinary, really, but the last to know it. But, I'm sorry...what can I get you to drink?"

"Don't be sorry at all. I never knew any of this, and believe me, my lips are sealed. A vodka tonic would do nicely, I think. Thanks so much for offering and for sharing all this with me. My Mariel needs and deserves to be happy...."

Rosie drifted in her thoughts, before resuming on a different topic.

"I must say, I never expected to stay here on the Island. I thought that Steve wanted to show us the city and all. I'm not complaining—don't get me wrong, but isn't this a change in plans? Or did he just want to do both?"

"He'll be here soon enough, and I'll let him explain his reasons. Steve is always full of surprises. Now, how about some herring to go with that cocktail, or perhaps some cheese? Let's go out on the porch. You really shouldn't miss the sunset."

Their peaceful banter continued until Steve and Mariel made it through the doorway well after darkness had clothed the evening in a cool damp coverlet. The weather seemed to be changing.

"Mom, oh, mom, it's so good to see you! What timing!"

Mariel warmly and tightly embraced her mom and rocked her back and forth.

"Mariel…you're crying! I didn't expect you to cry for joy just for this visit! It hasn't been *that* long has it, baby?"

"Mom, you have no idea. Your decision to come here right at this time probably saved my life!"

"What on earth are you talking about, and why do you look so serious? Mar…?"

"Sit down mom. Let me freshen up a minute. I'll be right back."

"Welcome Rosie. I'm Steve Irving. Please come near the fireplace. We have a lot to talk about. I'm so glad you're here."

Steve's hug was sincere even if a bit abrupt.

Taking a seat on an ottoman near the crackling fireplace, Rosie glanced at Steve, and back to Louie, and wondered why everyone seemed so solemn all of a sudden.

"What's going on, Steve? What did Mariel mean just now?"

"Louie, get her another cocktail, and bring me a double, too, please."

"Rosie, there has been an incident. It hasn't been sorted out yet, but it seems that a bomb went off at the hotel—on the same floor Mariel was staying on before you announced your visit. In anticipation of your arrival she had just moved a few of her belongings to a suite on the twelfth, floor so that you'd both be more comfortable. Soon afterwards, a bomb went off on the seventh floor where she had been. They evacuated everyone, and I just scooped her up and brought her here. Mariel is understandably shaken, but as you can see, she'll be fine. Rosie, I can't say that she would have been had she stayed on the seventh floor. It *was* good timing, but maybe we should put on the news."

"Oh... Steve! Mari...my poor darling, Mari...! Who would do such a thing? Did they catch whoever is responsible?"

Rosie jumped to her feet and was pacing.

Steve went over to the remote and immediately the large flat screen filled the room with breaking news. All the networks had the midtown Metro Towers, which had sustained a cavernous explosion and rather extensive damage, along with two fatalities, a dozen injured and two in critical condition—front and center in the news.

Most of the coverage loomed large on speculation and short on proof. It was just too soon. There was no one in custody for the crime, although the lobby cameras had revealed a possible suspect entering the hotel. An investigation was underway. The explosions had taken out the cameras nearest the detonated area, as well as shutting off others near the elevators and cutting power from those in the control room at the time of the explosion. The salvaged footage was being thoroughly reviewed for further clues. It would take hours before anything else would be known. Pictures of the two housekeepers who had been killed were revealed now that their families had been notified, along with eyewitness reports from guests who had been evacuated across the street.

Mariel winced upon reentering the room, to see the faces of the housekeepers she had come to know at the hotel.

"So…now you know mom," was her sullen comment. Continuing listlessly:

"What did the reporters say—any progress in the story?"

Mariel wrapped herself in a woolen throw and sat squaw-like on the couch. She was pale. She noticed how shaken her mother was. They both seemed to be in shock.

Steve sat right next to her and put a reassuring arm around her.

"Mar, you're safe here. No one knows you're here. What with the dogs and the gatekeeper, not to mention a very sophisticated alarm system, no one is getting within half a mile of you. We'll stay here as long as we need to. I won't let anything happen to you, Mar, you have my word. We will have to record a statement for the captain, however. One of my attorneys is drafting it as we speak. You can just read it when you feel ready."

"With a weak, but appreciative smile, Mariel looked into Steve's eyes. His devotion was tangible. How fortunate she was to have him. She did feel safe, for now at least.

"I'll have to get back to the city, so it looks as though I never left. We don't want anyone on our trail. Louie will stay here with you, as well as Ed at the gate. Rest up, my dear. Take a swim. Use the sauna. There's a gym downstairs along with a bowling alley, if you can believe that. The original owners were bowling champs. Hey, how about getting a whole new set of canvasses and paints sent up? This is a great place to paint, and you've been complaining about not being able to get back to it. There's a guest house on the southeast side of the property that would be perfect as a studio. You and mom can do a lot of catching up, even while you paint, right? How does that sound, beautiful?"

With his forefinger under her chin, he tilted her eyes up to meet his. His hopeful and generous offer was irresistible, and Mariel could not help but assent. She was too heady from the bourbon to protest anyway.

"That sounds great, Steve." She sounded a bit hollow. "But wouldn't it be easier to send someone to my flat in Boston, and just pack up my stuff?"

"Nonsense! You'll need it all when you get back there, and besides, it might attract attention. Just give me a list and I'll have everything overnighted right here. Be specific, because I know how fussy you are. I want you to have the best, so expense is not an issue. This will be just great! We'll get things sorted out about the hotel in a few days, and who knows, it could be totally unrelated to you. It's possible, you know. The only thing that bugs me is that the news shows will be all over me for an interview with you. I'll talk to our attorneys and get them to say that they've advised you to be silent, pending the investigation. *They* can talk to the media. That ought to work."

A moment later he was up pacing, and making calls.

Rosie stood up and went to the couch to buoy up Mariel, or herself, for that matter. She looked pasty and worried. Stroking Mariel's hair off her forehead, she leaned against her and tugged on the afghan.

"How about sharing, Mar?"

"Oh, sorry mom—I'm a little out of it. Here you go."

Steve jaunted back in the room with his coat slung over his shoulder.

"I'll be back on Tuesday, Mar. We can video-chat every day. Just move the laptop in front of a curtain or something so there are no clues as to whereabouts. Make sure you can't hear the ocean when we're on, or when you submit your statement to the police. Louie knows, and will help you. There will be more security guys here tomorrow. Ed knows them, so you don't have to worry. They will be positioned on the grounds. We have several gatehouses for them, so I'll keep them here as long as you're here. For now, Mar, stay on the property, ok? I don't want anyone recognizing you. In fact, we might need to give you a new look—cut and dye your hair, etc. What do you think? Rosie, perhaps you could help with that?"

Looking at Mariel, Rosie nodded silently while Mariel reached out once again.

"Sure Steve, whatever. But hurry back, ok? I feel a lot safer when you're here."

With a kiss on her forehead, he swirled around and headed for the copter pad, instructing Louie to be sure to provide them with every amenity imaginable.

Chapter Thirty-Three

Somber Truth

Mariel's head seemed to be spinning like the rotors which lifted, tilted, and swooped the chopper away a few minutes later. Two things had conspired to create an ominous storm cloud in her mind. First, there was the bomb. In all the rush—with Steve doing all the thinking—she hadn't taken in how close she had come to death or dismemberment. A bomb! It was an unwelcome visitation from a monstrous, mechanical, indifferent reaper. The reality of blown out walls, burn holes, smoke and death had repugnantly shattered her life before. Then, there was the term: video-chat. Why did Steve have to use the very words dear Sebastian had said? Wait! Steve shouldn't go back to his apartment or his office. He too could be targeted. She had to stop him.

"Mom, I've got to call Steve!"

A few minutes later, that worry was put to rest. He would stay in a hotel in New Jersey and could telecommute for a few days. Meetings would be offsite.

While it all should have put her at ease, somehow it didn't. This was all too familiar, except this time it seemed like a nightmare rerun so that she expected the worst to happen. After a few hours of just staring at the fire, and training their ears to the television for anything new, both she and Rosie were somewhat lulled.

"Mar...are you okay, sweetie? Maybe you ought to just turn in, take something to help you sleep and go to bed. How bout it? We're practically in a fortress here. Steve has left us well provided for and guarded. Maybe that's why, all of a sudden I feel as though I can't keep my eyes open. I didn't sleep at all last night from the excitement of the trip, and now, I guess, I'm tapped out."

"I'm so sorry about all of this, mom. This was supposed to be a celebration, and here we are...like chopped wood."

"Never mind chopped wood. We're together! It would have been unbearable for me *not* to be here. Can you imagine me turning on the television and hearing about it while all alone in my little condo? Don't you think twice about that! Tomorrow is a new day. We can see about that guest house, send off the list, maybe get some hair dye in here and get to work! Now, let me hug you, and how about it? Things always look better in the morning."

Mariel hugged her mom warmly and walked her to her room. She marveled at Rosie's ability to minimize every danger or impending disaster. Having endured so much already, each new threat seemed to arouse a familiar kind of resilience. It was how she coped.

It was not the same for Mariel. Whether it was the bourbon combined with winding down after so much pumping adrenaline, or just naked anxiety, Mariel felt as though she were facing a grotesquely ravenous tsunami that was just about to overwhelm her. Instead of drowsiness, she had a blurring, restless and wired energy coming from the sense of heightened threat. Her body was weak, but her mind seemed to spin and buzz erratically. She felt lost and without bearings, but not sleepy.

Chapter Thirty-Four

Raging Tempest and...

Throwing herself down on the bed and closing her eyes, as the dark and quiet of the vast, now vault-like mansion seemed to imprison her, she felt as though she were falling through an angry storm. Ominous winds tossed her at random as she seemed to spiral downward endlessly. She could not see anything in the writhing sting of this tempest. The feeling of confinement grew so oppressive that she sat up straight in the bed, breathing heavily.

With her mind exploding she instinctively thought of the balcony. She grabbed the afghan from the foot of the bed as she made her way there. Throwing open the doors, she stepped outside only to witness the exact mirror of her thoughts in the environment and weather.

The sea rolled and belched its inky depths. The moon was obscured by a thick layer of murky mist, which it still managed to back light in an eerie way as if some leviathan was spewing sickly fumes. Mariel was overcome with foreboding and inertia. Was she just a waiting victim? Would she have any warning of life's next tragic twist? Perhaps this *was* the warning of fate conspiring once

again to tear her apart. Perhaps she would...die! Having
escaped one blast didn't secure her from others, or from a
marksman or reeling car. It was cold outside, but with the
afghan draped around her like a tribal cape, she lay down
on the cushioned chaise lounge like passive prey in the grip
of a dominating predator.

With a sudden lurch, she seemed thrust into a raging
tumbler. Her falling speed seemed to accelerate, almost
unbearably. She would die at any moment.... A harsh
thunder clap shattered her ears and seemed to penetrate
her. Was she dissolving in the vacuum-like funnel which
mercilessly spun her as she continued her plunge? Was she
entering the very vapor that pressed and tore at her? The
overwhelming heat was disintegrating her...

"Mari...I'm here. Don't be afraid."

Was it really Sebastian, or just her thoughts? She
couldn't think clearly, and there was too little of her to
collect a response.

Then, in one startling, transforming instant, she was
wrapped in soothing puffs of gilded clouds, softly cushioning
every weary bone and sense. She bounced lightly as if on
tufted cotton bales, which restored and healed her with
every graceful surge. Swaddled in healing wraps of fragrant
air, she drifted lightly and safely on invisible paths. She was
restored. Although she slowly continued what seemed to be
a descent, all was bright and beautiful.

But...where *was* she?

As she drifted lower in a rocking pattern, much the
same way some leaves do as they gently find their way to
the ground, she began to see something below. Soft peachy
pinks with golden highlights formed what looked like the

most unusual landscape she had ever seen. Gentle mounds were covered in this magical garden of pink. As she grew closer, she realized there were roses—everywhere—a sea of roses more fragrant than anything she could imagine! Her soft and billowy transport placed her gently on a broad hilltop adorned with a myriad of roses! They were large enough for her to drift within, and as she did, she reached out to touch the velvet-like petals which enclosed her. Soft apricot, peach and pink were dappled with a tinge of honey gold the moment she made contact, and immediately she heard the unmistakable sound of childish laughter. Soon enough, peering out from the luxuriously draping petals— was a beautiful child!

With that twinkle of discovery in its eyes, the child smiled and waited for Mariel to speak.

"Well, you are a welcome sight. Hello. I'm Mariel. I don't think we've met."

A dozen faces peeked out all at once.

"Hello Mariel..." came the refrain, along with a new stream of giggling.

Then, the first child she had seen ventured closer.

"It is good to see you, too Mariel. We've been looking forward to this. The great Mother Queen told us about you."

"The great Mother Queen...? Not the.... Where *am* I?"

"You are in the realm of peace and bliss. Welcome."

"Am I alive?"

"Oh, yes. You've just come for a short visit, but we'll see you again when it's time."

"And what is your name?"

"Potentia. But please come with me. I am taking you to the great Mother Queen."

This gentle and calm place was more magical than anywhere she could imagine. Not a single thought of threat or danger disturbed the serenity here. Mariel followed the child, moving the petals aside like upside down draperies somehow fastened at her feet and freely flowing at the top. Clearing each plume-like petal aside, the jovial little group made a pathway that rose to a canopied area. Calming music accompanied by the sweetest singing surrounded her like a gentle breeze. The softly invigorating fragrance enveloped and wrapped her. A spongy golden moss, with a delicate sprinkling of glittering flowers filled Mariel with tingling exhilaration at each step. Countless cherubic faces welcomed her with great excitement as they ran ahead with little leaps and skipping.

And then...Mariel stopped...stark still.

The most exquisitely beautiful lady was reaching out a graceful hand—toward Mariel. Did the universe stop? Was there any sound, fragrance, or tangible...*thing* to compare with the consummate loveliness holding her gaze at this moment? Could she even breathe? Perhaps she *had* died.

So inspiring was that loving face, that Mariel felt the most restorative encouragement. The eyes she gazed into were like Caribbean jewels and more kindly and wide than a fawn's, more wise than any sage.

There were no words. The lady just smiled at her, and Mariel was embraced in tranquility. Looking into the lady's eyes, she understood. This was the great Mother Queen. All of the children who had suffered at the hands of others were safely loved by her. Their trials were like the blinking of an eye in comparison with the endless joy they would experience forever. In fact, those horrors did not exist anymore, but *they* would live forever!

Next, the lady extended her other hand toward Mariel. She held out a rose. In taking it Mariel understood that she had to let the shattered mothers of these children know: all was well. In spite of the dreadful mistakes they had made, their innocent children were preserved and both the Mother Queen *and* these children wanted nothing more than to let them know that mercy was theirs for the asking. Every dreadful act disowned would draw mercy down like a cleansing rain. Loving arms of healing and peace awaited them, beckoned them. The message went out and would not return without rescuing them. Their sins would be forgotten. If only they would trust. They were loved beyond all reckoning, and were awaited....

Now the Lady took Mariel by the hand, and turned her toward the most incredible light. It pulsed with life and goodness, and its rays brought astonishing insight with a depth beyond words. All would be well...all manner of things would be very well.... This too was the realm of the Great Lord who would see to it.

Chapter Thirty-Five

Back again

Three days had passed. Mariel had pneumonia from sleeping out on the cold, damp balcony that night. A fever had ravished her, but it was broken now, and she was waking.

"Mariel...Mari, sweetheart. You're going to be fine. We're all here." She felt a strong hand gently stroking hers. It was Steve.

"Your mother is here, and even Celeste is here. We love you Mari, and you're going to be all right, my dear. You're safe and you are loved. Do you hear me Mari?"

As her eyelids weakly fluttered, she saw Steve, then her mother, and finally, Celeste. Wondering if she might glimpse the great Mother Queen as well, Mariel was soon distracted by an annoying sting in one arm as she attempted to raise it. It was some sort of I .V.

All in the room breathed a collective sigh of joy and relief and hovered near to kiss and embrace her. Steve had a tear in his eye, and mom and Celeste were actually sobbing.

"Ladies, ladies, careful please...we can't smother her. Pull away a bit, and let her breathe."

As she tentatively surveyed her surroundings Mariel broke a subtle smile. Right there, literally filling the room were at least a dozen large vases of lovely blushing pink and peachy roses!

Chapter Thirty-Six

A New Look and Outlook

It was especially difficult to return to a world where a bomb threat had exiled her, but her mom and best friend promised a makeover to disguise her. Mariel's thoughts were unusually fresh. One thing was abundantly clear: She had to know who God really is. If she was about to die, she had to know what came next. Was she to join others in the wonderful realms she had visited or...imagined? She had to find out. Who exactly was the great Mother Queen? And... how soon could she paint and find a way to get the healing message she had been given—out to wounded women? She longed to talk to Fr. Leopold but was being kept quite busy by the attentions of her mother and Celeste. Other than that, she rested.

As soon as she was better, she succumbed almost indifferently to their insistence that she take on an entirely new appearance. Rosie went home for a few days but returned. It was an easy choice when her daughter needed her. The hospital obliged, and she didn't have to start for a month. At Steve's bidding, Celeste consulted her stylist who flew in to transform Mariel—after she had absentmindedly consented to this for one reason only—so that she could return to her own deeper thoughts and concerns. Gazing at herself in the mirror now, Mariel was jolted by her own reflection. With a shaggy, cropped style...and hair dyed...*burgundy*, Mariel was speechless! She had always kept her wavy hair long, and this seemed somewhat of a violation, albeit well intentioned.

"All I need are a couple tattoos and a piercing, mom. The color, Celli...how *could* you?"

"Actually, I think it's quite chic, Mar. You're thin and tall and short hair seems to sculpt you even more. You're just a bit more...cosmopolitan, really. I could get used to this," Celeste quipped as she brought over a pair of large, starkly serious glasses—minus any correction in the lenses—and poised them on Mariel's nose.

"Voila! The new beautiful!"

Considering the fact that she was truly unrecognizable, and it was all done, Mariel acquiesced. She was piqued, but uselessly. She might as well get on with things since it was too late anyway. Besides, no one she knew was going to see her this way, with the few intimate exceptions here, and maybe, even.... Realizing that perhaps this "disguise" might free her to see Fr. Leopold, Mariel found consolation in the hope that she could now address some of her burning questions. The ocean sun and air, along with fresh coffee and spiced nuts on the porch seemed to take the edge off. The three women eased into a friendlier conversation.

"Mom, I was so glad when I heard you'd be here."

She glanced at Celeste appreciatively.

"There were a lot of things I wanted to ask you, and I had hoped to celebrate with you. This incident has just sucked the life out of everything, but as you yourself reminded me, at least we're together. That part is great."

Celeste was wondering whether her presence might be awkward as Mariel shifted a little nervously. Deciding that this would be a good time to meet Louie's friend who was the dog handler and a guard on the property, she excused herself and left quietly.

"Well, I'm here, so ask away. What did you have on your mind sweetie?"

"Well, mom...am I...baptized?"

"Talk about a question! Wow, Mar, what brought that on?"

"I met a really kind priest when I was missing Sebastian terribly. I was feeling so lost, and stopped into a church. There, it seemed that I felt a presence—a calm and soothing one. When a priest stepped into a confessional near me, I just bolted right in...instinctively. I told him I wasn't Catholic or didn't think so anyway, but that I needed to talk. Mom, he was so wise and fatherly, and I've seen him a few times since. He gives me books to read and we meet to talk. When he asked if I was baptized, I honestly didn't know. Was I?"

Taking a deep breath, Rosie walked to the large screened porch from which she could see the soft foaming folds of gentle surf accented with swooping gulls, and quick stepping sandpipers.

"Mar, we have never talked about this and I'm feeling odd right now, like I was a bad mom or something. Your grandfather was a very religious man—you remember, don't you? When I was small, we went to church *every* Sunday, and he frequently marched all five of us kids to confession—Lord knows we had our share to tell. Your dad and I were married in the Catholic Church and promised to raise you Catholic. With all the moving around and your dad's deployments, it kept getting put off—the baptism that is—and then put off some more. Can I get you some water or something?"

"No mom, I'm fine. Go on."

"Well, that's it really. It would have been easy enough at Ft. Bragg, but I kept waiting for your dad to come home, and when he did we got caught up with the latest move we'd have to make. It just fell by the wayside. When it came to Sunday, to be honest, I just didn't feel like going to church when your dad was gone. He was the strong one. Then after Tom died, I just buried the whole issue. Prayer didn't save him. Meeting in a building didn't seem necessary. After all, I could talk to God anywhere at any time, but I didn't really want the company of the nosey bodies and all."

"So I was never baptized? What about Tom?"

"Actually Tom was, because we were more organized at the beginning. Your grandmother and grandfather saw us every weekend and it just fell into place. Things disintegrated when we moved to Florida and the moves that followed that one. Your dad continued his deployments, hoping to end them soon. Instead, Tom valiantly entered military service, and valiantly died in training. That knocked my lights out until you were born. You saved me Mar. I *had* to think of living—with a gurgling little baby girl to take care of! I'm afraid by then all church going had more or less been forgotten, except that your grandfather and Aunt Jean nagged me about it once in a while. So your dad and I would go to a dance or fundraiser, and I'd send in my baked goods, but that was about it. Then your dad tripped that roadside bomb…and well, it's been just us ever since."

"I guess I can hardly remember the last time we talked about any of this mom. You've had your share of tragedy."

"It made me the person I am, Mar. Marrying a military man, I had to learn quickly how to treasure what I *did* have, and not feel sorry for myself. My every day was like Disneyland compared to what the troops went through, or the civilians in those places infested with terrorist extremists. So, I learned to live—one day at a time. It's really the best thing we can do. And if we're still here, I guess there must be a reason."

"Dad would be really proud of you…being an LPN and all."

"Missing him doesn't bring him back, but I sure do miss him." Stretching broadly, and doing some stationary twists as well as head rolls, Rosie took a deep breath.

"So—why this sudden interest in baptism, Mari?"

"I want to look into it mom. I've seen enough tragedy. There has to be a reason. There has to be meaning. I'm beginning to understand that we see things so incompletely. It's like taking a piece of the universe—the size of a postage stamp—and saying that's all there is. When we get a glimpse of the vastness and beauty of the rest, even if only for an instant, our heart knows we were born for more. I'm feeling that way now, mom. I could never trust the search before. I had a kind of prejudice…snobbery really. I thought religion was just childish and myopic. You know—the old crutch. Science was so much more scintillating than a system or institution of prohibitions. After all, I'm an artist and freethinking. What a bunch of garbage! Regurgitated garbage at that! Lately, I'm seeing patterns of meaning which are impossible to ignore. From tragedy and disaster come the firebirds that rise from the ashes...what are they called...?"

"Phoenixes, I think." Relaxed and intrigued, Rosie looked at Mariel with new admiration.

"And that is what you truly are, Mariel, a firebird, a phoenix. I've seen you do it time and time again! You take your beatings but are not defeated. My brave and strong girl...."

The two hugged in silence. The admiration was mutual. They were both familiar with tragedy and violence in all its shapes and forms. They had survived a lot, and yes, it made them the women they were. These bonds could not be fabricated or undermined. Even if the mother/daughter relationship had its natural tensions at times, the women's identities were fused by shared experiences, especially, loss. They had enough freedom to be themselves, but remained always connected, and could respect each other deeply. They were ready to tackle some more of what life had in store. Realizing that the day was nearing its crescendo at sunset time, and that they were both a bit chilled in the changing and damper air, Rosie stood up to reopen the sliding doors to the house.

"By the way, every time I look at your new hairdo, I want a glass of Cabernet. How about it? Then, let's get Ed or Louie and take a walk on the beach to see the sunset!"

"That's it. Just call me cab head."

Their celebratory repartee was punctuated by the one

and only man who filled a room as soon as he set foot in it.

"What's this I hear about a walk on the beach, and calling a cab—all in the same breath? And...whoa, Mari... what did they do to you? Matzo balls and gefilte fish! Who on earth is this astonishing babe with the air of a Ph.D?"

Mariel was sheepish and awkward, having forgotten her new appearance.

"I think I let Celeste get carried away. Her stylist won some awards, but...."

"Mar, its perfect! You look...urban, artsy, and very... attractive, if I may. Quite a transformation, and just what we needed. The glasses take the cake!"

"So, I wasn't attractive before?" Mariel teased, feigning insult.

"I deserved that. Come on, Mar. You know how I feel about you. How about that walk on the beach? I've missed you! Celeste and Rosie, come along too. Where's Moxie? I didn't notice her when I came in."

"Oh, the vet is giving her shots and a bath," Rosie piped in. "They're downstairs."

"I'll call Ed. We'll use the south gate."

No one who saw them jaunting along the shore would ever have dreamed that a bomb had brought them together barely a week ago. Even Mariel felt that all was well with the world again, or clung to that feeling while knowing how precarious their situation really was. There was consolation in being surrounded by friends and family, although Steve filled a category all his own. Enjoying the Atlantic Ocean on a private beach certainly didn't hurt, either.

Chapter Thirty-Seven

At last, some good news

When they got in, a simmering dish of linguine and clams was ready to be served along with an arugula salad sputtering with roasted pine nuts.

"Tonight, we celebrate! They have someone in custody!"

A cheer and the clinking of wine glasses went up simultaneously. Talking all at once, each clamored to know the details and why Steve had waited until just then to tell them.

"Well, you know they had their suspects. No one in the line-up had a weak alibi. They were each let go after questioning. But now there's Fender—a marginal loner, with a cyber name of TerminatorNTwin, TNT—such an original thinker we have here! This guy can be traced to the purchase of bomb-making materials in Maryland and Delaware, where he lives. We have receipts all the way up the turnpike and in Manhattan. He had a hotdog a block away from the hotel, in the same hoodie we saw on the surveillance camera. He's looney and angry but so far has only a few misdemeanors. Did I mention he's not the brightest beam in the lighthouse? I take that back. He actually *is* intelligent, but drug use, especially coke, drives the erratic aggression he flares up with. When it does, he's too much in a hurry and makes all kinds of blunders. Equally unsettling is the cache of weaponry they found in his putrid apartment. Either he's a collector or part of a group. They're trying to figure that out now. Hopefully, the only twin involved is a multiple personality."

"When did you find this out, Steve?" Mariel looked penetratingly at him.

"Today Mar, just today. I wanted Louie—and Louie, this linguine is fantastic—to be with us to hear it, too. It's been rough on all of us, and I wanted us all to celebrate a breakthrough together."

After toasting Steve, they settled down to finish what seemed like a family dinner. Rosie and Louie were talking about the clam sauce, Celeste was telling Mariel about the apartment and the news from Boston. Steve looked at them all with a sense of deep satisfaction, and couldn't take his eyes off Mariel in her new guise. Nevertheless, there was a tinge of surrealism diffusing itself in the back of their minds and hearts. After all, Mariel could easily have been killed. Two innocent people had been, and everyone else was upset and shaken. Somehow, the rustic contrast between their ocean compound and the compressed city reinforced their sense of refuge and relief. Each of them clung to the serenity that their bond had forged, and a quiet and homey night passed as they gazed out at the moonlight licking the ocean-slicked shore and felt the salty breeze on their faces. As the fire in the outdoor pit dwindled and the mound of glowing coals seemed to be pulsing out some ancient code, they separated with hugs and each went to their room around midnight.

Chapter Thirty-Eight

Reality Check

Shortly after Mariel had pulled up the satin sheets and plush blanket, she could hear Celeste tapping, and in the pale glow from the nightlight saw her as she pushed open the door and came directly over to Mariel.

"Mar, are you up for some midnight ramblings? I know I won't sleep."

"Sure Celli. Drag that chaise lounge over just a bit, and you'll be more than comfortable. It's as good as a bed, really. Hey, I'm glad you came. Aside from turning me into a cab head, this has been great. You've always been a true friend, Celeste. It's really great to have you here."

"Of course, Mar. You'd do the same for me unless you were in one of your slumps or obsessive painting spells...." She gave Mariel a reassuring side hug before settling on the chaise.

"You're right, Cell. You come to my rescue more than I can ever come to yours."

"Well this time I'm scared, Mar."

That was all it took. The illusion of security and

tranquility had just been sucked out of the room as if a soundless funnel cloud had touched down.

"Me, too, if you don't already know. It was just too close. Once they identified my room as the actual detonation site, I knew that this was probably a focused and deliberate attempt to kill or at least scare me to death."

"What are you going to do? You can't just stay here forever. And even if you did, well...you could be...well, it could be discovered and publicized."

"Oh, come on, Cell, I'm not that famous. On the other hand, you're right about not staying here forever. I was hoping that now—with the Fender guy in custody—perhaps we could plot a strategy. There will be a trial and all. I sure hope they get some solid information from him...and a possible connection to Sebastian's research."

"Mar, that kind of thing can take months or longer. If you go back to the city, I'll bet one of the tabloids will pick this up. Ever since those celebrities came to the exhibition, you're one by association it seems. I'll bet they're sending flowers already. You watch. "

"Not here, I hope! I hadn't thought of that. Knowing Steve, he's probably sending out some sort of misinformation about my whereabouts. I hope no one from the hotel knows that I'm here. I did meet a few of the year round residents there, but not enough for them to know my comings and goings nor I to know theirs. Some of Steve's associates or friends—you know how many people he knows—seem to live there. I met a few at a cocktail party that Steve insisted we go to, since they are big supporters of the ICC."

"Mariel, who would have thought that any of this would happen...I mean, really? It wasn't that long ago that you were back in Boston painting the most amazing panels and called me up so that you wouldn't have to show them to Steve alone. Now you two are like...an item. "

"Careful, Cell.... It's not quite like that, but I do have to admit that I find myself relying on him more and more. It wouldn't be a balanced relationship when you add it up, though."

"Mar, it doesn't get much better than Steve Irving, as far as I'm concerned. He is really devoted to you, and well, he's got every asset along with your passion to save kids from trafficking. How great is that all rolled into one man?"

An uncomfortable silence filled the room. Celeste sensed it was the usual shield that went up in her dear friend whenever the suggestion of anyone taking Sebastian's place was made. She left Mariel to her thoughts.

"Celli, I'm confused about it all, really. I know how lucky I am to have Steve. I've gotten to the point that I'm always wondering what he would want me to do in every new situation. That's exactly what worries me. Am I losing myself in the process? Does this dependency mean I've somehow fused my identity with the man who has saved me in so many situations, and has in fact brought me along during my grieving for Sebastian? I do wonder sometimes whether I should allow myself to string him along this way. On the other hand, I really do need him, and have grown... well, comfortable with that, especially since he's so willing. It's confusing, really."

Sitting up cross legged and leaning in towards Mariel, Celeste looked sympathetically at her.

"As usual...Mariel is conflicted. Maybe you're just

complicating things too much. Think about it, Mar. You've gone from one major heart-pounding event to another—the exaltation of success, the crashing reality of near death—and it doesn't get any more dramatic than that. I think you need some down time—some quiet, uneventful, painting time. Let it all just filter...you know, sink quietly into your head and heart, and you'll know where you stand. I think you're close to a new threshold."

"I haven't told you about this, Celeste, but I've been seeing a priest."

"Well, *that's* a segue, and not one I saw coming! Most friends would say, well I'm seeing this guy, or that guy, but you, Mar, are seeing a priest! What do you mean...what for?"

Drawing herself up against the headboard as she propped up a few pillows, Mariel seemed to revive a bit.

"I feel really drawn to...well, the Catholic Church. It's weird, Celli, and there's a lot to the story, but I truly have a desire to be baptized. I can't even explain it, except that I believe...it's hard to talk about—but it seems that God is in this—as if he's leading me... and it brings me a lot of peace to follow that...lead, if I can call it that."

"Wait, you're saying that God is leading you? I don't get it. Where does the priest come in?"

"You mentioned earlier how I can find myself in a slump. Well, that's no secret. It's on and off with me since I lost Sebastian, and it happened in New York sometime after the exhibition at the Metropolitan. I charged out onto the city streets late one afternoon, and later found myself in St. Vincent's Church. I don't know why, but when the priest went into the confessional, I followed."

"You went to confession?" Celeste was all ears.

"Well, not exactly. For some reason, I felt...drawn. My grandfather mentioned it to me a few times, and even though it sounded really scary when I was a little girl, I remember how reverently he spoke about it. It was something that he personally experienced and benefited from. So that day, when I needed to talk to someone, I decided to talk to a priest."

"So you went in the box? Mar, this is unbelievable! Weren't you—I don't want to say scared—but hesitant?"

"I told the priest I didn't know how to go to confession but just sort of poured out my troubles. In the process, I must have mentioned my paintings or something because he realized that I had painted the Gem Babies and told me that I should continue to paint. He told me I had a gift and needed to share it. As it turned out, he had gone to the exhibition since he's an art lover. Then, he recommended that I make an appointment so that we could talk some more— outside the confessional."

"Wow. I'm Catholic and I didn't know priests did that."

"It was really because I was looking for guidance that he offered to continue. Confession is mostly for getting sins off your chest, but I wanted guidance, and he said that it might be better to talk some more when he could give me his undivided attention. It did make sense when I slipped out of the box, since there were actually a few people lined up who were waiting to speak or confess to him. I had no idea people did that."

"Unbelievable, Mari. I'm stunned...to my core. Mariel, you truly are something else. You went to confession! That's something I never expected to talk about tonight, but it's great, really."

"It is truly amazing. Fr. Leopold has really inspired me. He's very kind and gentle, and I really do feel drawn to pursue baptism. I want God to be a part of my life."

"Have you told Steve? I'm just curious about how he would react. He's Jewish, isn't he?"

"We haven't really talked about religion at all, but, yes, he is Jewish. My mom told me that Louie told her what a moral person he is, which we all know anyway. I don't think he'd interfere in any way."

"You know what, Mariel? You've got the best support system ever! Incredible! And you know what else? I think I could actually sleep now. What do you say? I'll go back to my room so I can brush my teeth and all, but this has been great. Good night and sweet dreams. You just never cease to amaze, and I sense a really cool twist in the story of your life ahead. If I'm not up for breakfast, don't bother me, ok? I feel ready for a little extra sleep if that's okay. We can talk some more tomorrow."

With a wilted stretch, and after a haphazard side hug, Celeste meandered wobblingly toward the door.

"No worries, Cell. Ciao."

Chapter Thirty-Nine

Frustrated

The next day Mariel woke up restless. As she came down for coffee, she discovered that Steve was already out running with the dogs. Celli was still sleeping. Her mom's room was empty, and there was no word about where she might be. The temporary studio wasn't ready for her yet. What would she do with herself?

Soon enough with mug in hand, she went out on the porch to breathe in the morning air. She looked out at an overcast sky and a calm ocean. There was a tone of suspense in the way that sea and sky combined. Thick with expansive and inflated-looking, gray clouds, there was no blue to be seen on water or sky. A storm might be coming, but it was difficult to tell any direction of wind or movement. The stage was set, but there was no starting cue.

A line from Julian came to Mariel's mind. It had resonated the first time she had read it, and it seemed like a tolling buoy now. "He did **not** say you would not be tempest tossed, or work weary. He said you would not be overcome." The double negative had caused her to reread it several times when she first came upon the turn of phrase. Being familiar with inner turmoil and a driving desire to work at her craft, it appealed to her. It calmed her. At least, it served as a reminder that while the storms might rage and howl, she would not be swept away. However, this could be the calm before the storm, a reality she was becoming all too familiar with.

Just then, Louie and her mom came up the lawn from the direction of the shore.

"Honey, I didn't expect you up this early. Louie was showing me around and we ran into Steve with the dogs on the shore. Have you had breakfast?"

Noticing the mug, Louie brightened up.

"So you found my coffee. It's never too hard with the aroma of deep, dark Italian roast."

A cymbal crash and trumpet blast ring tone sent him whirling toward the phone.

"Uh... who's calling please? I know a neighbor who had a temp with a name something like that working for her on planning a summer banquet, but I'm not sure about anyone else. We had considered hiring her, too but learned that she had gone to Paris for culinary school or something. Yeah, a nice girl...Marina, or Morela, or something. What is the purpose of your call? Maybe that will give me an idea of where to send you next."

Mariel's innate alarm system was on high alert. Louie was obviously trying to avert a caller who had given her name. Who on earth could know she was here? Her heart was pounding.

"Father Leopold? Well, I don't know father...it seems you might be calling the wrong number...."

"Louie, is it for me? I know Fr. Leopold. Let me take the call!" she gasped, trying not to shout.

With a stern shaking of his head, Louie had no intention of allowing her to take the call.

"Well, how bout this father: let me get your number, and I'll see if I can turn up a connection for you from my neighbor here. How does that sound? Hold on, I'll have to get a pen...just hold on, okay?"

"What are you doing, Louie? I **know** Fr. Leopold, but no one knows that I do. It should be safe even though I have no idea how he got this number. I want to talk to him."

"No way. I was briefed about this kind of thing. Even if he's legit, we can't be sure about bugging or something until the wiring team comes. Listen in from the patio phone and at least we'll know if he's who he says he is."

"With a ruffling of some papers, Louie was back on the phone, pen in hand. Go for it father. What is your number?"

A broad smile swept over Mariel's face as she recognized her dear fatherly friend. When Louie had hung up, Mariel rushed back in the room.

"It's him alright, Louie, and I'm dying to talk to him.

Mariel shot him a chastening glance. "But, I really don't get it...how did he know I was here?"

"He doesn't necessarily *know*." Louie was solemn and pensive. "Steve's number is forwarded here when he wants it to be, and apparently that is what happened. All Fr. Leopold had to do was call the ICC office and they would connect him to Steve. They don't know anything at the office and think that Steve has been in the city the whole time. Who would refuse a priest anyway? Steve probably set it to ring here while he was on his way back. Apparently Fr. Leopold just took a chance that you might be with Steve."

"Can't I call him back or at least call the church?"

"Mariel, look at me sweetie. Steve would have my head and rightly so, if I took any chances that could compromise your safety. For now, this is the best deal going—having you out on the island—and I'm not going to be the one to jeopardize it. Steve should be back from his morning ritual soon. The wiring guys are coming, and I could easily buy some temporary phones for the house. Once we get the "all clear" you can go ahead and call the priest, okay?"

Mariel drew a long staggered breath. She was beginning to feel so trapped and caged. It was an uncomfortable, but familiar feeling.

"I'd like to go out to the casita, if that's okay. Just to make some sketches...all right?"

"Sure, sure—no worries—but please don't leave the compound without one of us with you, okay? I'm sure you'd have way too many invitations for a drink from our curious neighbors. Deal?"

"Okay, Louie. I don't really want to see anyone, believe me."

Chapter Forty

Unwelcome Surprise

With that Mariel headed out to the casita, one of three actually, reserved for special guests. This was the jewel. It had the best view of the shore, with two stories, and a great porch for gazing. As she climbed the three stairs to the porch and opened the creaky screen door, she heard the back door slam and could see a vague figure through the kitchen window. Fumbling with the key to the main door for a moment, she entered anxiously and ran to the back window. She could see a barefooted man in rolled up denims, running with an unbuttoned long sleeved shirt flapping in the breeze and some sort of shoulder bag.

"Now, that is weird, and I'm not liking it one bit," she thought. Rather than explore the casita for other intruders, she hurriedly locked the front door and rushed back to the house. Happily, Steve had just returned with Moxie and Tumbler. He looked exhilarated and happy. He came right over and gave her a hug, noticing that her preoccupied look didn't match his.

"Why so...worried?"

"Steve, I was just at the main casita. As I opened the

front screen door, I heard the back door slam. When I got inside and looked out the back, a barefooted guy was running from it with a black shoulder bag."

Quick to respond, Steve speed dialed his guardhouses, and whistled to Moxie, who happily pounded outside right after him.

"I want all of you out inspecting the entrances and walls. We have a barefooted, unaccounted-for male on the premises, and I want him caught. He has a black shoulder bag and I want to know what it's got inside."

Sure enough Moxie picked up the scent and trailed the man as he was trying to throw a repelling line over the top of the wall. She had him pinned, and though usually a warm and friendly dog, she had her growl on and teeth bared.

"Good girl, Moxie!" Two guards rushed to Steve's side to restrain the man.

"Just what on earth were you doing *on* my property and *in* one of my guesthouses just now? Who are you?" Steve barked.

There was something vaguely familiar about the man who was young, small of stature and clean shaven, but Steve couldn't pin it.

"Larry, call the police."

He didn't look at Larry but burned his stare into the intruder as he tried to remember where he had seen him before.

"So far we've got trespassing along with breaking and entering, and we've just met. Who knows where this is going? Bruce, cuff him. You've got the authority. Link him to that iron bench over there until the cops come. Larry, go to the main gate to let them in."

A few minutes later, the sirens were nearing the compound.

Pacing as he stared, Steve knew he had seen this man before.

"So you're not talking, eh? Who are you and what did you *think* you were doing here?" he demanded.

"Ok, I'm a freelance *photographer slash paparazzi.* I heard that Mariel Turner was here and jumped at the opportunity. After the bombing at the hotel everyone is trying to figure out where she is, and with the tip I had, I was about to prove it in pictures."

"Well, your career is over hotshot, if I have any say about it. What gives you the right to trespass and break into one of my guest houses? I'll see to it that you have the book thrown at you! Who gave you that tip anyway?"

"That, I can't say."

As he looked at the rather frightened young man in front of him, it became clear! This was the rookie cop he had paid off at the rear of the hotel the day they left. But how did he know where Steve was going? Realizing that he had only used the chopper *after* the initial trip out here, he called Louie back at the house.

"Louie, I want you to...yeah we got him. Stay there with Mariel and make sure she doesn't leave your sight. Listen, Warren is in the garage waxing the hummer. I want you to get him to look the Porsche over with a fine tooth comb. I have a feeling we picked up a tracking device in the city. Call me if he finds anything, which he probably will. Tell him NOT to touch it until we have it dusted for prints. The cops are here and I want this creep booked!"

"Officer, this man was caught on my property without our invitation or permission, and he broke into one of the guesthouses. He threw that repelling hook and rope over the wall and was attempting to escape when we detained him. Bruce here is part of my security team, and I asked him to cuff the guy. We're checking to see if he planted a tracking device on one of my cars, which would have been the only way he'd know to come here."

Just then, his phone rang.

"Bingo!" It was Louie.

"You were right Steve, there's a device under the rear bumper."

"Good job, Louie."

Clicking the phone off, he made a triumphant turn to face the policeman.

"Officer, we've discovered an unsolicited device on one of my cars, as I suspected. Would you like to have a look? I want it dusted for prints. Do you have someone who could do that, or should I have Bruce do it? You should know that he is a bona fide P. I. whom I retain in my security crew here."

"So that it doesn't come back to haunt you later, Mr. Irving, I think one of our guys should do it, but thanks. I could almost hear it now...what we *don't* want to hear at the courthouse: 'evidence is tainted and we request it be withdrawn on the grounds of planting and incrimination of the defendant.' Know what I'm saying? You don't want that, so give me a minute, and I'll call it in. We're going to need pictures *and* prints at the guest house, the wall, and wherever else our friend here went anyway."

"How about we get some coffee at the house, officer? The garage where I keep the car is near there, and the guards at the gate can direct your guy to the main house."

Casting a sardonic glance at the handcuffed intruder, the policeman answered, "I think I'll secure *him* in my patrol car, where he can sit pretty while we have our coffee. Can I drive you up, Mr. Irving?"

"Sure, officer...I didn't even catch your name...oh, Tompkins," he affirmed, reading the name badge. Is it okay for the dog to ride along too?"

"I don't see any reason why not."

Once inside, Louie had warm croissants out with farm butter, scrambled eggs and Canadian bacon, cheese, fruit, and of course, wonderful coffee.

"You know, Officer Tompkins, you could actually add impersonating an officer to his charges."

With his cheeks swollen with the buttery croissants, Tompkins could only manage a muffled "Oh?"

"Yes, I might as well tell you. When the room that Mariel had been staying in was bombed, I rushed over to the hotel to get her out. Knowing the chief of police on a first name basis because of my work at ICC, I had clearance to take her away and supply a statement later. By that time, however, the police were in force, with guest lists for everyone and patrolmen posted at the entrances and exits. Or so they thought. They did not take warmly to my claim of clearance from the top, and started delaying things. I did not want her stuck in the city after this attempt on her life, and I'll take my lumps for this, but I told her to exit out the back where I'd pick her up in my car. At that moment, it seemed unguarded. All I had to do was move my car from the front of the hotel to the rear. When I got there a few minutes later, there was a "policeman," after all with a clipboard and list. Guess who it was? You got it! He was in uniform so the patrol thought that exit was covered, and so did I! That's probably how he planted the device on my car! I noticed him at the rear of my car taking down my plate numbers as I bolted toward the door for Mariel so that I could let her know I would use a phony name to get her out. At that point, my back was to him. Returning toward the car and sheltering her as much as I could in my overcoat, I pushed a $100 bill (or was it more?) into his palm for the Police Athletic League and told him we had the misfortune of choosing the hotel that day to meet for coffee and that she wasn't a guest. He took the money, and pretended to clear the name I gave as he thanked me and urged me to hurry away. That creep had just the time he needed to plant that tracker under the rear bumper just when my eyes and mind were on Mariel! He had us as we pulled away, and we never suspected a thing!"

Chapter Forty-One

Catching a Breath

Steve seemed exhausted but peaceful as he reentered the breakfast area, about 30 minutes later.

"Well, Mar, I think we can breathe easier now. Officer Tompkins just rolled out with a certain Sam Wengel. He'll be booked for trespassing, breaking and entering *and* impersonating a police officer. That's for starters. I think this guy is even dirtier. Let's hope his prints outlasted the drive from the city here—on that tracking device he planted."

"I am relieved to know we got him, and that they have enough to keep him. Do you think it will go to trial?"

"If my instincts are right, they'll get him on the tracking device, too. They also took his camera so he'll have to explain the pictures—none of which I got to see."

"Did he really break into the casita? I didn't even notice. I guess I was too afraid to look anywhere but outside to see who it was."

"Oh, he was good. He did a perfect cut to the glass on the door. We wouldn't have heard it if we were *inside*. Then he reached in for the knob. He seems to have experience.

What a creep. I wish we could book him for the $100, but that could be more incriminating for me, so perhaps it's better not to play that card for now. Come here, Mar. I need to tell you how much I care for you and how beautiful you are—in the worst of circumstances. I promise, as soon as this blows over, we'll get away for awhile. How does that sound?"

"Frankly, Steve, like a pipe dream. The investigation could take months or a year, then a trial, then sentencing. I see at least a year and a half, and that could be rushing things. What if he gets off or has a short sentence? What about others who are out there? We don't even know who we're up against. I don't see a vacation any time soon."

"Let's be optimistic Mar. We've got the bomber and this creep. This cloud has a silver lining I'm telling you… this could be the break we've been waiting for."

Pulling away a bit thoughtfully, Mariel turned demurely back to Steve.

"I was wondering, Steve…now that my disguise is so convincing…do you think I could see Fr. Leopold, or that he could come here at least? He called for me, but Louie wouldn't let me take the call."

"I know. He told me, but we got so busy with the break-in, it's been on the back burner. I'm sorry, Mariel. He's like a father to you, isn't he, Mariel?"

"Even more than that, Steve—lots more."

"Louie will set up some temporary phones, like we do when I have friends from Europe or South America visiting. We keep the number for a month, pay our bill, then throw out the SIM card, and recycle the phone. Ask him for one of those, and you can go ahead and call Fr. Leopold. We had his place checked for bugs and he's clear. That place is so antiquated in technology, I think they still had corded phones! But Mar, if only for a little longer, I'd rather that he came and stayed here, than you go into the city."

"Yeah, I think I would, too. I hope he can. He'd probably love it here. I'm going to find Louie now."

"Oh, and Mar... don't step out anywhere alone, okay? I'm still a little jittery from this incident."

"Does Moxie count for company? Just kidding, I won't, Steve."

And with a warm hug, she went to call Louie. In a compound of this size, it saved a lot of time.

Chapter Forty-Two

A week later

Sitting down to dinner with Fr. Leopold, who was now a part of their household, brought a sense of blessing to Mariel and peace to everyone else as well. Steve had no trouble warming to him, as he recognized a true man of God in this serene and humble, yet very learned and sensitive man. They had much in common with their love of art, and sharing their firsthand experiences with the greatest galleries in the world.

It was around ten in the morning two days after Fr. Leopold had arrived, when Steve came back from his shoreline run with Moxie. He was just in time to answer the phone with an energized and cheerful:

"Good morning, Officer Tompkins. Have you got some news for me? Make it good, okay?"

Then, with a series of: "you're kidding..." and "no way!" and "Jackpot!" type exclamations punctuating the conversation, the broadest smile of relief and happiness bannered his already beaming face. When he got off the phone, he looked up, said his two favorite words in Hebrew, "L'chaim" and called everyone to the breakfast area.

"Fr. Leopold, Mar and mom, Celeste, Louie...ok listen up, this is really good! Grab a cup of coffee and sit yourselves down. Do I have news for you! "

Excited chatter and speculation were percolating. No one wanted to wait, but Steve insisted that everyone have a little to nosh on and sit down before he would share the news.

"Just now, I got off the phone with Tompkins. Well, in short form—we hit the jackpot with Sammy, it seems. His camera and apartment had the worst pornographic photographs. Some were plainly of minors, even young children! It seems Sammy was a small peon in a prostitution ring that trafficked children, teens and women from South America and Eastern Europe. Once here, they were basically sex slaves and lived under the constant threat of beatings or death. Many were hooked on drugs to keep them willing and "productive." It seems that this particular ring has ties to Chechnya, and had a vested interest in wiping you out as a warning to any others who might attempt to disrupt them. What brutes! As if...! Once law enforcement collected the evidence, Sammy started singing like a canary hoping to save his own neck. It seems like he'll be going up the river, and they'll be throwing away the key. The most he could bargain for is a more comfortable mattress...*maybe!* One of his names even knows Vorona... remember the black crow from Russia whom we suspect is kingpin? This is big, Mar, really big. I think this is finally the vindication we've been working for!"

As far as the TNT guy goes, they're not sure he knew who was paying him. He's a loner creep recruited from his deranged website and a cellmate who listened to

219

his insolent rants while they were both doing time for assault and battery connected with a serious robbery. So it wasn't just the misdemeanors, as I had been led to believe. Nevertheless, he somehow got out in six years after that. That won't happen this time!"

Tears and shouts were raining down as each one held the one nearest them in the tightest of embraces. Even Louie grabbed onto Fr. Leopold.

"You brought us luck, Father! This is great! In fact, I want to go to confession...today! I feel God walking right back into my life!"

Celeste was choked up.

"I was thinking the same exact thing. I can't believe it! Ever since Mari told me she went to confession, it's been eating at me. I'm Catholic, too, but...well...I don't even know how long it's been, father. I just want to pick up where I left off..." Now she was weeping with joy and contrition.

Mariel held Steve tightly. It was really because of him. She was so blessed to have someone like him in her life, and she was beginning to open herself up to all that possibility might mean for the future, with Fr. Leopold's help.

"What's going on here?" Steve interjected. "This is supposed to be a celebration, and everyone is crying! How we got from apprehending a real criminal to confession, I guess I'll never know, being a good Jewish boy. But this calls for a celebration, and we're breaking out the bubbly for some mimosas, or straight up if you like. Louie, how about some bagels and lox to go with it? That will be quick and easy! And, one more thing....

Mar, I told you I wanted you to have a break when we

could. Well, we can. In fact, the secret service is involved now that it's gone international, and they are suggesting we leave the country for a span. That gives us a few months at the very least. Now, here's what I had in mind: how does a tour of the world's greatest art galleries and places of beauty sound to you? The Louvre, the Prado, the Tate... every inch of Florence, Rome, Assisi—pick your favorite and we'll see it! Throw in Monte Carlo, Lake Como and then Geneva and Zurich, Salzburg and Prague! And here's what I'd like to do: you *and me*, Mar."

Realizing there could be overtones, he quickly turned to Fr. Leopold and Rosie.

"Now, it will be on the up and up...adjoining, but separate rooms. We'll share a wall, that's all—you have my word of honor. And what's more, I'd like to sponsor Fr. Leopold, whose knowledge of art far surpasses anyone I have ever met, and who speaks both Italian and French fluently. He has confreres throughout Europe and could touch bases while he's there as well. What do you say, Mar...?"

He had his arms around her, but at a distance this time, as he waited for her response.

"How could I possibly refuse? Steve you really are *too* good to me"

"Nonsense, beautiful—that isn't possible!" And after an embrace and full lift and spin, he set her down again, all smiles. "Fr. Leopold, would you honor us with your company?"

"Steve, you are too generous. I will have to ask permission of the community. However, if I kept a journal, and did some research there, I think I could swing it. I've been hoping to get into the Vatican archives for some time, but lacked the opportunity and sponsorship to do my research. If I publish articles, hopefully I could inspire the faithful, as well as benefit the community monetarily. This sounds like a win-win to me, and you have *my* word—he said with his winning smile—I'll give it my best shot!"

"And speaking of shots, I'm pouring! Who's in?"

Flutes were clinking, conversation flowing, hope sprung out of every weary heart, and for now at least, it seemed that all things were well, indeed *very* well.

The End of Book One.

CPSIA information can be obtained at www.ICGtesting.com
Printed in the USA
BVOW07s2158111113

336027BV00001B/1/P